THE HILLS HAVE EYES

"There's a lot of wild horses in this country," Sheriff Benton said. "Mustangers have been coming here for years, but the country proves so tough that they usually ride out busted with fewer sound horses than they owned before leaving town. I guess the sole exception to that rule is Keana."

"Who?"

"We call her the Mustang Maiden! The woman is a complete mystery. She's like a ghost, but she's as pretty as an angel. A dark angel maybe, but an angel all the same."

Longarm shook his head. "Ed, you're piquing my curiosity."

"In this case, curiosity is about all that you will ever have. Keana never shows up at the same place at the same time. She's crafty and knows this country like the back of her pretty hand."

"Any chance that we'll see her out here?" Longarm asked.

"The chance of that happening is slim. Keana and her kid might be watching us right now, but we'd never know it. That's the way they want it to be. They see . . . but remain unseen."

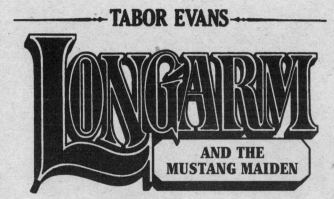

TABOR EVANS

LONGARM

AND THE
MUSTANG MAIDEN

JOVE BOOKS, NEW YORK

LONGARM AND THE MUSTANG MAIDEN

A Jove Book / published by arrangement with
the author

PRINTING HISTORY
Jove edition / February 2000

All rights reserved.
Copyright © 2000 by Penguin Putnam Inc.
This book may not be reproduced in whole or in part,
by mimeograph or any other means, without permission.
For information address: The Berkley Publishing Group,
a division of Penguin Putnam Inc.,
375 Hudson Street, New York, New York 10014.

The Penguin Putnam Inc. World Wide Web site address is
http://www.penguinputnam.com

ISBN: 0-515-12755-8

A JOVE BOOK®
Jove Books are published by The Berkley Publishing Group,
a division of Penguin Putnam Inc.,
375 Hudson Street, New York, New York 10014.
JOVE and the "J" design
are trademarks belonging to Penguin Putnam Inc.

PRINTED IN THE UNITED STATES OF AMERICA

10 9 8 7 6 5 4 3 2 1

Chapter 1

United States Deputy Marshal Custis Long sat very still in the saddle, watching and listening as he held the reins of Sheriff Ed Benton's restless gelding. The wind was blowing hard and whipping so much dust across this high desert country that Longarm didn't see how Benton could possibly read tracks, but the man had already brought them this far on the outlaws' trail.

Benton looked up. "Well, Custis, there is no doubt in my mind that they know we're following them and that they'll set up an ambush sooner or later."

Longarm studied the rough Nevada country with its endless crumbling rock, deep arroyos, and tall sage. It was a harsh and empty land not worth visiting and certainly not worth living in for any period of time. And yet, he knew that there were isolated cattle ranches out in this mostly empty land where the Ruby Mountains drained into the desert. There were also wild mustangs and wilder men who preyed upon the scattered ranching and mining towns of the region. Since Longarm was a federal marshal, that was Sheriff Benton's concern rather than his own. However, when those same outlaws decided to start killing United States mail clerks and stealing mail, then it became a federal crime, and that was why he was here now.

"You still think there are five of them?" Longarm asked.

"Maybe six," Benton replied. "But, if I'm reading these tracks right, one of them owns a lame horse. See this track?"

"Faintly."

"Well, it shows that one of the animals is limping pretty badly. My guess is that this deep track indicates that two of 'em are riding double."

"So how far are they ahead of us?" Longarm asked.

"Not more than a day." Benton checked his cinch and decided that it needed tightening. He was a thick slab of a lawman in his middle forties with prematurely graying hair and a pronounced lameness, courtesy of an old bullet wound to the hip. Custis had met him at the train station in Elko and they'd hit it off pretty good. Benton was a professional like himself and he didn't talk too much . . . or too little, which meant that he said what was necessary and kept quiet when there was nothing to talk about. The man was an excellent tracker, but he admitted to being short-sighted.

"Custis, I can read just fine, but I've learned from experience that my eyes aren't so sharp anymore for distances," Benton had explained soon after they'd taken up the trail of the ruthless Haskill Gang. A gang led by Chance Haskill, who had sworn never to be taken alive and returned to prison, where he and his younger brother Eli had already spent more than half their murderous lifetimes.

"I need to know *exactly* what you can see," Longarm had told the man. "It could mean life . . . or death, if we are ambushed."

"You're asking me if I can see a man in rifle range and I have to say that I cannot," Benton had admitted. "At least, I can't if he fires a high-powered rifle."

"What if he has a Winchester carbine?"

"That's tough to say." Benton frowned. "Depends on the light and if he's wearing clothes that stand out."

"An outlaw probably won't be," Longarm reminded the man. "Are you a good shot?"

"Now, I am that!" Benton said proudly. "With a pistol or a rifle. Don't you worry about me not holding up my end of this manhunt. I've arrested more outlaws than I care to recall and I've had my share of tight fixes. All I'm telling you now is that I can't see real well to the distance, especially if the light is in my eyes."

Longarm had understood and appreciated the man's forthrightness. It was far better to know these things to start with than to find them out after the shooting began. So they'd left Elko with enough supplies to last them two weeks, providing they were able to hunt fresh meat. The trouble was, Longarm hadn't counted on the weather being this cold and raw in June, so he hadn't brought a heavy enough coat, a pair of gloves, or even woolen underwear to keep him warm in his blankets when the temperatures slipped down into the freezing range each night.

Benton finished tightening his cinch and remounted. His bay gelding was nervous and difficult, especially on cold mornings. The sheriff had explained that he liked the animal because it was a "goer and he never quits," but Longarm thought the gelding was a pain in the behind. It continuously threw its head around, and no matter how many miles they traveled, pranced and acted foolish. No doubt that it was fast and tough, but a dancing, excitable horse was dangerous on the outlaw trail. In contrast, Custis's buckskin was a sensible animal that watched its feet and kept its head down and minded not to accidentally step into a hole or off the narrow trail in this difficult country.

Longarm waited until Benton was remounted, then let the man lead off toward the northeast again. Having the better eyesight, Longarm felt that it only made sense that *he* should be in the lead in case they were being set up for an ambush, but the stupid bay gelding was too excitable and competitive to be happy following his buckskin, and insisted on being in the lead.

3

"I think the gang is headed up into the Ruby Mountains," Benton called back over his shoulder. "That's where there are plenty of canyons and pines, water and grass for their horses. I wouldn't be surprised if the Haskill brothers have relatives that run cattle in those mountains."

"That's bad news," Longarm called. "It means that we not only face the gang, but probably a bunch of their family."

"I know," Benton agreed, "but that doesn't change the fact that they killed two federal postal employees in this last train job, and you have to bring the gang in dead or alive."

"You're damn right," Longarm replied. "It's just that, had I realized we might be facing an entire family, I might have wired Denver for some additional help."

"Oh, hell," Benton called back over his shoulder. "We'll do all right. Are you pretty good with a gun and rifle?"

"Fair to middlin'," Longarm said modestly.

In fact, he was an *expert* with both weapons, and several more that weren't being mentioned. But a man was always foolish if he began to overestimate his self-worth. Custis had seen more than his share of good and bad men get overconfident and then get killed. His philosophy was to expect and be prepared for the absolute worst because, in his line of business, it happened more often than not.

They rode for another three hours, and there were times when Longarm could not see even a hint of the outlaws' trail because of the windblown dust and sand as well as the hardness of the ground. Mustangs, coyotes, rattlesnakes, and lizards might like this country, but it was certain that it would prove tough taters for a farmer. Still, there was an undeniable beauty out here and now, as the sun began to set, he caught sight of a band of wild horses far off in the distance.

"Mustangs!" Longarm called. "Looks like a pretty large band."

"There's a lot of wild horses in this country. Mustangers

4

have been coming here for years, but the country proves so tough that they usually ride out busted with fewer sound horses than they owned before leaving town. I guess the sole exception to that rule is Keana."

"Who?"

"We call her the Mustang Maiden!" Benton twisted around. "She's as wild as the mustangs themselves and a whole lot prettier. I've only seen her in Elko a few times. Keana keeps entirely to herself except for that Paiute boy she seems to have adopted a few years back."

"What does she do?"

"She's a mustang hunter and a hell of a lot better at it than any man. She only catches quality horses, none over three years old, and she even tames and breaks them to saddle before she delivers them to town."

"Isn't that pretty unusual?"

"Damned unusual," Benton agreed. "Most mustangers will set up relay teams and run their prey into the ground, often killing the weak, old, and younger horses just to catch and rope the strong ones. That doesn't make sense to Keana, and it doesn't make sense to me either. When she brings a band of mustang ponies into town for sale, the buyers come around in bunches, and they know they're going to get top-grade animals and are more than willing to pay for it."

"What does this woman do with the other mustangs she catches?"

"Turns 'em loose, I suppose. The woman is a complete mystery. Some fellas have tried to get 'friendly' with Keana, but she don't give 'em so much as the time of day. That's why the cowboys in this country have nicknamed her the Mustang Maiden."

"And they leave her alone?"

Sheriff Benton shook his head. "I've no doubt that a few of them have tracked her and that Paiute boy hoping to take advantage, or at least learn her mustanging tricks of the trade. I've also had folks come upon bodies out in the brush, and I'll bet the Mustang Maiden has killed more than a few men to protect herself and that boy."

"She sounds like an original," Longarm said.

"Oh, she is! I don't know where she came from and I don't know where she mustangs, but I expect she casts a wide loop. She's like a ghost, but she's as pretty as an angel. A dark angel maybe, but an angel all the same. Most people agree that she's at least part Indian, although she is taller than any Paiute woman I ever saw."

Longarm shook his head. "Ed, you're piquing my curiosity."

"In this case, curiosity is about all that you will ever have. Keana never shows up at the same place at the same time. She's crafty and knows this country like the back of her pretty hand."

"How old do you think the woman is?"

"Twenties. It's hard to tell, though. She might be older . . . or younger. I do know that she loves her mustangs. You'll never see one showing the signs of having been mistreated. The townfolks who buy her horses say you can put children on their backs—they're *that* safe and well broken."

"And she doesn't have any family?"

"Not that anyone knows about. The Paiute kid—and I forgot his name—is about ten or eleven years old. He's a cripple like me, only his limp is even worse. Some say he was ambushed by other mustangers taking target practice on anything that moved. Others say the kid was hurt by a mustang, and still others believe that he fell into a snake pit and was bit all over the legs. I don't know. He's like most Indians . . . real quiet. When he is on the ground, you think he's not much of anything or anybody. He sort of swings that bad stiff leg like a club. But when he is on a horse you get a whole different opinion, because he rides bareback and you swear he is part of the horse. I've seen that kid race mustangs through heavy brush; he's a horseman you will never forget. If you ask me, it's the kid

6

that manages to overtake the wild horses and that's Keana's secret to catching them when others are left behind."

"Any chance that we'll see her out here?" Longarm asked.

"The chance of that happening is slim. Keana and the kid might be watching us right now, but we'd never know it because that's the way they want it to be. They see . . . but remain unseen."

"Do you think she knows the Haskill Gang?"

"No doubt about that," Benton reasoned. "She must have had plenty of run-ins with that outlaw gang. Keana would hate them because they are bloodthirsty killers. I've heard that they beat and rape women and shoot mustangs just for sport. They're evil, and Keana would not want to have anything to do with such cold-blooded men."

"I'd think she'd have no choice."

"Ah," Benton replied, "but she *does* have a choice. You see, this country is so empty that there's plenty of room for folks to keep to themselves, if they want. Besides outlaws and the Mustang Maiden, we have prospectors and trappers, but they always keep a fair distance from each other."

They rode another couple of miles before Benton pointed out a shelter up under some high rocks. "That will make us a good camp out of the wind."

Custis was plenty ready to call it a day. As a federal deputy marshal, his job was to track down criminals of all types, but that was often done in towns and cities, so he spent a as much time in railroad coaches, stagecoaches, and other public conveyances as he did in the saddle. He liked horses and getting out in the wilderness, but he wasn't as saddle-hardened as he would have liked to be, although that might change on this difficult and dangerous assignment.

He and Ed Benton didn't waste time wondering what to do when they made camp. Right from the first, they'd each taken on the small tasks that were necessary to care for both themselves and their horses. Benton preferred to cook and he was good, so Longarm had gratefully taken on the cleanup chores. He also performed most of the packing and unpacking because the sheriff seemed indifferent to that important task and his bad hip made ground work difficult.

"It's not going to be as cold tonight," Benton said as Longarm dumped an armful of wood for their cooking fire under the rocks. "I haven't been able to figure out why you didn't bring a heavier coat, though."

"Try stupidity," Longarm cryptically replied. "I didn't realize that the nights got so cold out here this time of year."

Benton sorted through the wood, putting some aside and carefully building a little pile of selected branches for his starter fire. "That's the high desert for you, Custis. Out here it never fails to get hotter than hell in the summertime and colder than an old cow's titty in the wintertime. Same for individual days, when it can reach a hundred degrees in the afternoon and then drop all the way down into the forties or fifties at night."

"I wouldn't like that."

"You get used to it if you live out here long enough," Benton said, nursing his fire until it was going good. "I came out from Texas in the year of fifty-six to make my fortune mining Comstock silver up in Virginia City. When I crossed this particular stretch of desert, I swore that I'd make my money and return to Texas as fast as was humanly possible . . . but I never did."

"Why not?"

"I don't know," Benton replied. "I lived on the Comstock Lode for years and was a hard-rock miner. We'd be lowered down a deep shaft in a wire cage into the bowels of mighty Sun Mountain. We'd pound and blast rock eight or nine hundred feet underground, and we earned five dollars a day, thanks to our miners' union. But it aged a man in a hurry, and I couldn't stand up to it like some of the Welshmen whose families had done it for generations. Besides, I was always afraid of being buried in a mine cave-in or explosion, which happened all the time. I did manage to save up some money, and then I got a job as a deputy marshal in Gold Hill and discovered I had a knack for the work."

"How's that?"

"Well," Benton said, "I'd always been good with a gun, but even better with my mouth. So I learned I could generally talk a fella out of his foolishness. In the five years I was a Comstock Lode lawman, I only had to kill five—no, *six* men. Now, that might sound like a lot, but it wasn't because of the wealth and the wild times. You ever been up to Silver or Virginia City?"

"Yes," Longarm said, "but not in their heyday. By the time I arrived, the mines were mostly shut down and there wasn't much activity left on the Comstock."

"I know that," Benton said, shaking his head with regret. "Mining towns come and mining towns go. They rarely last as long as a miner's dreams. Anyway, when the good times ended, my job ended. I had married, but my wife ran off with a fella who actually did make a small fortune in mining. Last I heard, they were living it up in San Francisco. I don't blame Emma for going away with a wealthy man. No, sir. I was poor and determined to find another law job and you know our line of work is short on pay and long on risks."

"You ever remarry?"

"Nope. And crazy as it may sound, I still consider myself married to Emma." Benton chuckled, but the sound was forced and without joy. "I'm a romantic fool, you see."

"Who knows," Longarm replied. "Maybe Emma will return."

"Naw! Won't happen. But there is this spinster woman that lives only a block south of me in Elko. Her name is Louise Martin. She's skinny and has one bad eye that circles like a moth around a flame, but Louise possesses a sweet nature and good heart. I go over to see her every Saturday night. I cook us supper and she reads Shakespeare to me later on in the evening. When we get to a really romantic part, Louise gets excited, so I take the book from her hands and we have a good time in her big, four-poster feather bed."

Longarm shrugged. "Sounds okay to me."

"It *is* okay. And I really believe if I asked, Louise would marry me."

"So why haven't you asked?"

"I'm afraid she'd run away like Emma." He heaved a big sigh. "To be blunt, Custis, I just don't trust women anymore."

"Not all of them will run off with another man just because he has more money, importance, or health. Women are as different as men. I think Emma was just plain fickle."

"Yeah, but she was a beauty! My wife reminds me a little of the Mustang Maiden I told you about."

"Is that a fact?"

"Yes, except that Emma wasn't as tall and didn't have that long, straight black hair falling nearly to her butt. My wife was kind of short, but she had breasts that would make a milk cow turn green with envy . . . and eyes that melted my heart."

"How long ago did she run off with the Comstock mining man?"

"She left me eight years ago."

"Try to forget her," Longarm advised. "How old are you?"

"Forty-four."

"How old is Louise?"

"She's three years older, but she's frisky as anything in bed."

"Marry her," Longarm said. "She sounds like a find to me."

Benton winked. "You seem hot on me getting hitched, but I haven't heard you speak of any Mrs. Custis Long."

"That's because she does not yet exist."

"Why not?"

"I just haven't had the time or energy to marry. One day

I'm here, the next somewhere else. I am on the go nearly all the time, although I do keep a room in Denver near the Federal Building, where I work. The thing is, I always seem to be on the outlaw trail, and that is no kind of life for a married man."

"So find a new line of work! You're still young."

"I like what I do," Longarm answered. "I am good at it and I can't imagine doing anything else."

"Me neither. Louise and I have talked about me giving up my badge and taking a town job. She owns a little cafe and . . ."

"And you like to cook!" Custis grinned. "Sounds perfect!"

"Might be," Ed replied with a wink. "But compared to this line of work, it'd be pretty boring."

"Compared to this line of work it would also be a whole lot healthier," Longarm reminded the man. "You are getting to the point in life where you ought to quit this business. Your eyes are telling you the same as I am—give it up."

"You getting hungry?" Ed asked.

"Sure am."

"Me too. Guess we'll be having rabbit stew again tonight. Maybe tomorrow we can shoot something different to put in the pot."

"Such as?"

"Rattlesnake meat is as tasty as fried chicken."

"I don't know about that," Longarm told the man. "Perhaps we can move up into the pines and get us some venison."

"That sounds good to me!"

Longarm and Sheriff Ed Benton enjoyed their supper while watching a fiery sunset. Then, they checked their horses to make sure they were secure for the night, and climbed into their bedrolls.

"I hope we catch up with this gang tomorrow and put a finish to them," Ed drawled just as Longarm was falling asleep. "They need to finally be brought to justice."

"We'll try to arrest them first," Longarm replied. "We only kill 'em if there is no choice."

"Oh, there won't be a choice. You can bet on that! Chance and Eli would shoot it out with the devil himself before they'd surrender. Mark my word, Custis, we'll either come out with five or six stiff bodies . . . or we won't come out at all."

Chapter 2

They awoke at dawn, and Longarm was shivering in the cold. There wasn't much daylight on the eastern horizon, just a faint salmon-colored glow. Longarm drew his knees up to his chest and tried to get warm. At least, he thought, the damned wind wasn't blowing. After ten futile minutes of trying get comfortable, he climbed out of his bedroll and fumbled with matches and wood. The fire was as reluctant to come to life as he was but he got it started and then made coffee, using water from his canteen. This had been a dry camp and he knew the horses were thirsty. Sheriff Benton had promised they would find plenty of water up in the Ruby Mountains, and Longarm hoped they'd do it before noon.

He fed the horses, and when he returned to their little rock shelter, Benton was astir. The older man was surprisingly cheerful. "Custis, how'd you sleep?"

"I've slept better."

"Me too," Benton said, climbing out of his blankets. "But I've also slept worse. I remember one time I was chasing a murdering skunk who had gunned down an old man for his mule. Anyway, it was a long, hard chase up into Idaho, and damned if it wasn't in the middle of winter. But I remember that the weather couldn't make up its mind if it

13

wanted to rain or snow. You ever had to camp out in sleet?"

"Yeah. In Colorado."

"Then you know what I'm talking about," Benton continued. "Sleet turns to slush and you quickly get wet and miserable. To make matters worse, the murdering skunk was heading into high mountains, and I knew that I had to stop him before he got into deep snow. As it turned out, I nailed the bastard with a buffalo rifle at a distance of at least four hundred yards. He was flogging that mule with a quirt and trying to get through a pass, but I got him in my rifle sights and drilled him in the back. Only bad thing was that the slug went through his body and hit the mule in the neck, killing it too."

"You just shot him like that?"

"I had to! If the bastard had gotten over the pass he was as good as home free because all his kinfolk lived on the other side. It was him . . . or me."

"What did you do with the body?" Longarm asked aloud, wondering how the sheriff had explained a huge bullet hole in the man's back and the dead mule.

"I didn't do anything! If the mule hadn't been killed, I would have got it back for the old man's widow. But since it was dead and I knew the man's killer didn't have but a few dollars and an old Navy Colt pistol, I didn't even bother with the body. I figured that the wolves or bears would eat the carcasses long before spring thaw and that would be the end of the story."

Sheriff Benton shook his head and warmed his hands over the fire. "Man, but that was a cold, hard hunt!"

"What did you tell the old man's widow when you returned?"

"I told her that the mule and the killer drowned trying to cross a big frozen river. I said they broke through ice and just disappeared. Then I paid her ten dollars out of my own pocket because I felt responsible for her not at least getting the mule back." Benton fished a frying pan out of his pack, then some salt pork, which he sliced. Using a

14

little fat and lots of salt and pepper, he set the meat to cooking, and found a couple of potatoes to add to the breakfast. "I also felt awful because that mule was a really damned fine animal."

"Some mules are better to ride than horses," Longarm said. "They're more sensible and surefooted."

"Of course they are. They're far smarter."

They talked about mules and horses until breakfast was ready. "You make the coffee awful strong," Benton said.

"That's the way I like it on the trail."

"Louise knows how to brew a good pot of coffee. We have breakfast together on Sunday and Wednesday mornings. She always goes to the bakery and buys me some pastries because she knows I enjoy them so much."

"Marry her," Longarm muttered.

"I might . . . someday."

"Don't wait or she could find someone better."

"I've thought of that, but she scares men off with that one wandering eyeball always circling around and around. Doesn't bother me much—especially in the dark in her feather bed—if you know what I mean."

"Sure I do," Longarm replied.

"I'll just bet." The sheriff winked. "A big, handsome stud like you who makes a lot more money working for the feds than us local yokels has got to have women chasing him all the time. Bet there are some real pretty ones in Denver. Huh?"

"There are," Longarm admitted. "I should pack so we can get moving."

"I guess. It's still pretty cold, but the day ought to warm up and the wind has finally died. I just hope we don't wind up the same way."

"Yeah."

Longarm wasted no time packing and then saddling the horses. Benton was really hobbling, and Longarm guessed that the cold, hard ground took its physical toll on the sheriff. Benton, he thought, ought to find an easier line of work.

They climbed into the pines, and now Longarm could plainly see the tracks of the horses they were following. This was high, lonesome country and abundant with wild game. If they knew that the Haskill Gang was beyond hearing rifle fire, they'd have shot a young buck and had venison to pack by now.

Sheriff Benton's excitable gelding was acting up on the steeper parts of the trail, and Longarm could see that the man was getting upset, so he called, "Why don't you let me ride ahead?"

"Ah, that's all right. This stupid sonofabitch is bound to wear down soon."

"I'm not so sure of that," Longarm replied. "And if we suddenly get jumped or come under fire, you don't need to be fighting that bay gelding."

But the lawman was stubborn. "I can handle him. Let's just keep our eyes peeled for trouble."

Longarm was trying to do just that, but it was hard with Benton's horse prancing and jumping all over creation. The animal had been difficult down in the desert, but now it was impossible. *I'd shoot the stupid sonofabitch if he was mine,* Custis thought.

They stopped at noon and rested by a spring. The horses drank deeply, and the air was cold but still. Longarm kept his Winchester close at hand and his eyes moved constantly, searching for danger. Overhead, a blue jay gave them a piece of his mind, and Longarm pitched some pieces of sourdough bread to a bold ground squirrel.

"I never been to Denver," Benton said. "Like to someday."

"It's really growing fast. Too fast."

"Yeah, I prefer a small town like Elko. We got the train coming through most days, and that always brings news from both coasts and strangers to gossip about. In the fall, the local ranchers are shipping a lot of cattle out from the stockyards and the cowboys are feeling flush with money. That's when my job is busiest, but I don't mind. Over the years, the cowboys have learned that I have certain boundaries and rules they cannot break. If they respect those, they'll be okay and we won't tangle. I have more trouble with the whores, pimps, and gamblers than I do with the cowboys."

Longarm was only half listening when he saw his buckskin suddenly raise its head to look up the mountain. The blue jay went silent, and just as Longarm was about to offer a warning, a rifle shot shattered the stillness. Sheriff Benton had been standing facing Longarm, and now he was thrown forward. Longarm grabbed the man just as a second rifle exploded. He fell back on the pine needles, and then scrambled to pull the wounded man into the thick cover of rocks and manzanita.

"I'm hit bad!" Benton wheezed. "Jesus, I think I'm going to cash in my chips!"

Longarm gently rolled the man over and saw a dark stain of blood widening on the back of the sheriff's coat. At the same time, Longarm was desperately trying to keep a lookout for the hidden riflemen. "I've got to pull your coat and shirt off and try to plug up the bullet hole," he hissed. "If I don't, you're sure to bleed to death."

"Don't worry about me, I'm a goner! Take cover and defend yourself, Custis."

"It doesn't work that way," Longarm said. "But I would appreciate your help in getting your coat off."

Benton gulped; his face was already losing color. "Just kill them ambushing bastards. Do that and I'll die a satisfied man."

"Shut up!" Longarm tore the man's coat off and then rolled him onto his stomach. Yanking up his flannel shirt, he saw that the rifle bullet had shattered Benton's shoulder, but probably had missed the lungs or any other vital organs.

"I'm done for, ain't I?"

"No, you aren't. Just hang on because I'm going to plug up the bullet hole and try to stop the bleeding."

"There's no time for that. Don't you understand that

they'll be coming in on us? They know I'm a dead man."

"No you're not. You're going to help me . . . aren't you?"

"If you think I can."

"Then be quiet and still. If we can fight them off, you've still got a chance to marry skinny Louise . . . wandering eye and all."

"You're a crazy man," Benton choked, already sounding weak as Longarm pressed his bandanna into the man's wound and then used his belt to tighten it and staunch the bleeding. "And I still say I'm a dead man."

Longarm rolled the sheriff over so that his own body weight placed pressure on the makeshift bandage. "Here's your six-gun. Stay still and quiet. I'm not waiting for them to come for us. I'm going after them."

"Against five or six expert killers? My gawd, man! Get to your horse and ride for your life!"

"Keep talking like that and I'll finish you off myself," Longarm grated before he began to move deeper into cover.

Longarm had learned from long and painful experience that the best thing to do against a numerically superior enemy was what they least expected. The Haskill Gang would expect him to try to escape with his life . . . not to attack. Some of them had most likely circled around and cut off his backtrail down this mountainside, and were waiting to drop him as he retreated. Only Custis *wasn't* going to retreat. He had a rifle and maybe even the element of surprise. They'd be overconfident, and that meant he had at least a small, temporary advantage.

He stayed low and moved carefully until he arrived at a large fallen log. Then, he eased down under its mossy underside and waited for several minutes until he saw two of the gang members approaching cautiously from behind trees up the slope.

"Come on. Come on," he whispered, pushing the rifle out in front and then taking aim. "Just a little closer."

The first man was big-shouldered and wore a dirty

sheepskin-lined jacket. He was followed by a short, stocky fellow wearing a derby hat and with an unlit stogie clenched between his teeth. Longarm laid his sights to rest on the larger of the pair and squeezed off a round. Even before the big man grabbed his gut and doubled up with a scream, Longarm was already swinging the barrel of the rifle toward the second man and levering in a fresh bullet. He shot the stogie man in the back as he was running for cover. The fellow crashed through the brush and thrashed for a few moments before he lay still.

"Two down and only a few more to go," Longarm hissed, moving back toward Sheriff Benton so that he could protect the wounded man.

A moving shadow appeared off to Longarm's left, and he swung the Winchester and fired in one smooth motion. He heard a yelp, and then received return fire from three directions. Longarm threw himself behind a rock and waited as the rifle fire echoed off the mountainside and down into a nearby canyon.

"Chance! Are you hit!" someone called.

"No! Are you!"

"I'm fine, but the bastard drilled Ollie and Pete! He's hiding up in those rocks! Let's get him!"

"Yeah, boys, that's right," Longarm said to himself, "come and get me."

He heard the sound of a Colt, and knew that Sheriff Benton was defending himself. Longarm jumped up and charged through the brush, hearing bullets clip the nearby vegetation. When he reached Benton, he grabbed the wounded sheriff and pulled him deeper into cover. The sheriff moaned, but did not complain.

"What the hell is going on!" Longarm panted. "Who is shooting at you!"

"Nobody. I just figured that they needed an extra lawman to worry about. I figured that they might decide I was dead."

19

"Better that you had pretended to be dead and then drilled an unsuspecting one."

"Don't give me any more grief than I've got already," Benton breathed. "I feel like I'm standing on death's doorstep."

"You're going to be all right, if we can get you to a doctor soon enough to dig a slug out of your shoulder."

"Damn few doctors in this neck of the woods. I'll settle for taking a couple of these mangy coyotes with me."

"I never seen anyone so eager to cash in as you are," Longarm replied as a bullet whined off the rocks just inches from his head.

"Best keep your head down," the sheriff advised.

Longarm hugged the ground. "I got two right away, but the rest will be tougher. Any suggestions?"

"Nope. They aren't likely to call it quits until we're finished."

"Or they are."

Longarm checked the bandage. "The bleeding has stopped. Do you think you can move?"

"Sure. But why?"

"They're closing the noose on us," Longarm replied. "If we can break out, then we have a better chance."

"We got to get to our horses, Custis."

"That would be nice but I doubt that's going to happen if—"

Longarm saw an outlaw jump from cover and open fire. He returned his own fire and the outlaw staggered, then disappeared.

"Did you get him?" Benton asked hopefully.

"Winged him, I think. Maybe he's finished. I don't know. It's dark under these trees and hard to see clearly."

"I have to say this," the sheriff told him with unconcealed admiration. "You are one hell of a good shot. Keep it up and we'll be headed back to Elko as a couple of heroes."

"That'll be the day," Longarm said cryptically. He settled in to wait for the next target, but it did not come.

"What do you think they are up to?" Benton asked after a long time had passed.

"I think they will try and creep in close after dark and finish us off," Longarm told the man.

"Can you get to our horses?"

"Hell," Longarm answered, "they're gone."

Benton cussed. "I'll never make it out of these mountains on foot."

"I know that."

"Well, then?"

"I'm thinking." Longarm frowned. "They know exactly where we are. We need to move just as soon as it is dark. I'll take you down this mountain fifty or sixty yards, then creep back and lay my own ambush."

"Sounds good."

"I hope so," Longarm told his friend. "I'd like nothing better than to finish this up tonight."

"Me too."

So they waited. Benton was in a lot of pain, but his color improved, and Longarm was encouraged by his stamina and newfound will to survive. When dusk began to fall, they went over their plans again. Longarm ended up by saying, "We just need to move you forty or fifty yards. No more."

"Then let's go," Benton told him. "It's dark."

It wasn't easy half dragging and half carrying the wounded man out of the rocks. Every second that passed brought increased danger and vulnerability. Longarm was almost certain they'd be heard and then seen and then shot, but the bullet never found them. And when they reached another outcropping of protective rocks, Longarm eased Benton down and caught his breath.

"How we doing?" Longarm asked.

"I've felt better, but I'm alive."

"And you'll *stay* alive if you just do what I say."

"I'm listening."

"Keep very still, but keep your six-gun up and ready to

fire. I'm going out there and try to bring the odds down in our favor."

"But it's so dark. How will I know if it's you or them when you come back?"

"I'll . . . I'll whisper your name."

"Can't you do better than that?"

"Any suggestions?"

"Sure! Make the sound of a big owl. You know . . . *hoo-hoot!*"

"I'll try."

Longarm edged back and then began to crawl on his hands and knees. Darkness had fallen quickly and completely. He could barely see the stars above, and the overhang of pine boughs blocked out what little moonlight there might have been.

He heard movement and froze.

"That you, John?" someone called.

"Yeah," Longarm grated.

"Where are they?"

"Dunno."

"Don't move and I'll come to you. I can't see shit!"

Longarm waited and when the speaker appeared, he raised his hand and brought the barrel of his Colt down hard across the man's skull. The outlaw collapsed on the pine needles and didn't move again.

Now we're getting down toward even odds, Longarm thought with grim satisfaction.

He waited for someone else to make a mistake. An hour passed without sound or movement. Finally, a faint voice called, "Chance, what's going on!"

"Don't know. Everyone sound off!"

"Bert here!"

"Eli here."

A long pause, and then. "Who else! Call out, dammit!" Silence.

"Holy shit! Let's get out of here!"

Longarm came to his feet and tried to find a running

target, but failed. He heard confused shouting, and then the drumbeat of flying hooves in the forest. Too late did he race after the last of the outlaws, knowing that the fight was over but that the game was lost without horses.

Chapter 3

Longarm returned to Sheriff Benton feeling angry and discouraged. "How are you feeling?"

"I've had better times. What about the Haskill Gang?"

"I shot at least two . . . maybe even three. The rest took off with our horses."

"Then we're sunk," the sheriff said flatly. "Because the ones that got away will go up into these mountains for reinforcements. I expect that they'll be back in force within twenty-four hours. Maybe longer, maybe quicker."

"Yeah," Longarm replied. "I'm going up the mountain to do a body count. Sit tight."

"What choice do I have?"

"None."

"Be careful," Benton warned. "If you've wounded any, they'll try to nail you from ambush. Shoot first and ask questions later—that's the way to handle these vermin."

Longarm made sure that his gun was reloaded before he went to find out who among the gang was dead and who was still alive. Moving cautiously because there might be a wounded outlaw waiting to drill him, Longarm made sure not to offer an easy target.

The first outlaw that he came upon was the big man in the dirty sheepskin-lined jacket, who lay staring up through sightless eyes at the overhead branches of a pine. Longarm removed the man's cartridge belt and pistol. He checked all his pockets for anything that might give him a clue as to the body's identity, but the only thing he found was a good Barlow knife, which was always useful. Longarm removed the sheepskin coat from the big man and wiped away the stains of fresh blood. The coat fit well, but it was filthy, and he hoped it carried no lice.

The shorter man he'd brought down from behind was also dead. He'd dragged himself nearly fifty yards into the brush, leaving a trail of blood to mark his path. He was armed with a pair of well-oiled pistols, which Longarm confiscated. But again, the man carried no identification.

"You boys better hope that your friends return to bury you because I haven't the time or the tools," he said in parting. Longarm started back down the hill, but heard a moan and spun around with his six-gun up and pointed.

"Help!" a weak voice pleaded from the cover of heavy brush and rocks. "Don't leave me to die!"

"Come out with your hands up!" Longarm ordered.

"I can't. I'm hurt!"

"Then I wish you a speedy trip to Hell," Longarm told the outlaw as he backed away. He had no intention of walking into the man's trap and getting killed for attempting to be merciful.

"Please help me, mister!"

"I am Deputy Marshal Custis Long and I'm placing you under arrest. Come out with your hands up or I'll leave you to die."

Longarm heard the sound of branches snapping. A moment later, a tall, thin young man with blood still pouring down his face appeared. Longarm recognized him as the one that he'd pistol-whipped. The outlaw was bent at the waist and cradling his head in his palms. As he staggered down the mountainside, Longarm expected a trick, but the outlaw was really suffering and offered no resistance.

"What's your name!"

"Moses."

"Moses what?"

"Uh . . . Moses Smith."

"You're a liar," Longarm growled as he searched his prisoner's pockets for concealed weapons. "Keep your hands up until I say you can put them down."

"Marshal Long, my head is broken! I'm seeing double and I think my brains is comin' out my ears! You got to help me."

"The hell I do," Longarm snapped.

When he was satisfied the outlaw was unarmed, Custis told him he could relax. Moses took that to mean he could collapse. "Oh, man, my head *really* hurts! You got any medicine?"

"No."

"What about whiskey?" Moses looked up, eyes blood-shot and pleading. "I got to have *something*!"

"Get on your feet and start down the mountain," Long-arm ordered. "You're lucky that I'm a lawman and can't finish you off right now."

Moses climbed shakily to his feet. He was well over six feet tall, but probably didn't weigh even close to two hundred pounds. He was sharp-featured with a hooked nose and pointy chin, his hair, scraggly goatee, and mustache the pale, yellowish color of watery piss.

"Mr. Lawman, I didn't do nothing wrong. Honest!"

"You don't call ambushing me and Sheriff Benton doing something wrong?"

"Well . . . we didn't know exactly who was followin' us so we had to protect our backtrail, that's all."

"Tell that to a judge and see how many years it will earn you in a federal penitentiary," Longarm replied, jamming the barrel of his Colt into his captive's spine. "Now move!"

Moses complained all the way down to where Sheriff Benton was resting. When the older lawman saw the prisoner, he sat up and spat out, "Well, well. If it isn't Moses

Haskill, better known as Weasel. How you feelin', Weasel?"

"My head is near broke, but I probably don't feel any worse than you."

Benton glanced at Longarm. "Any other vermin still alive up there?"

"No, but I found two dead. One was a big fella whose sheepskin coat I'm wearing."

"That would be Bill," Weasel whimpered. "Did you also plug a short guy with a cigar in his mouth?"

"Yes. What was his name?"

"Ernie."

"I want their *last* names."

"Bill Case and Ernie Ware." Weasel looked to Benton for help. "You've heard of them two, haven't you!"

"Yeah," the sheriff replied. "I sent them to prison about ten years ago for cattle rustling and for beating a sheep-herder nearly to death. They deserved to die."

"Well, I damn sure don't!" Weasel grabbed his head and moaned as if he were dying. "Oh, I think my brains are coming out my ears! What am I going to do?"

Longarm could see blood trickling from both ears, and realized that Weasel's skull really was cracked. No wonder the outlaw was in such pain.

"What are we going to do?" Benton asked. "I got a slug in my shoulder and Weasel will try to kill us at the very first chance. We've no horses and Chance and Eli Haskill are damn sure going for help."

"Maybe so," Longarm told him. "But we are both still alive and able to put up a good fight."

"Yeah, but I'm not going to be able to put up much of one."

"Sheriff, you'll do fine when the time comes." Longarm glanced up at the night sky trying to figure out what time it was. "We have to make some hard decisions and we have to make them right now."

28

"Our only chance is to hide." Benton took a deep, ragged breath. "That is, unless we split up."

"What does that mean?" Longarm demanded.

"It means that you should leave me and Weasel and try to reach Elko. If you tell them what happened, you can form a posse and return. Might only take you five . . . maybe six days."

Longarm shook his head. "We both know that by then you'd be dead."

"So?" Benton stuck out his jaw. "Better just me than the both of us. If you return with a posse, then wipe the gang out! Kill every last one of the sonofabitches!"

Weasel raised his head, and for the first time, he seemed to really understand what was being decided. "Mister," he told Longarm, "if you leave me behind with Benton, he'll kill me before sunup. Let me go with you."

"Don't listen to him," Benton snarled. "He'll be waiting for the chance to catch you by surprise and return the favor by caving in *your* skull."

"I'm not listening to either one of you," Longarm told them. "What I do know is that we have to move right now and keep moving as long as possible. They'll expect us to go back to the high desert and retrace our steps toward Elko. If we do that, they'll catch us sometime tomorrow morning."

Benton frowned. "But—"

"Sheriff, do you know *anybody* that lives around here we can trust with our lives until we shake the Haskill Gang?"

"There are prospectors and trappers in these mountains, but most of them are probably in cahoots with the Haskill boys and would betray us the first chance."

"Well," Longarm told the man, "that's the chance that we have to take. Let's go find help."

"There ain't none for fifty or a hundred miles!" Weasel cried. "And anyway, I hurt too bad to walk."

Sheriff Benton yanked his six-gun out of his holster,

cocked back the hammer, and pointed it at Weasel. "I'm glad you made this such an easy decision."

"No!" Weasel shrieked, falling to his knees and clasping his hands together. "Please don't kill me!"

"You'd have killed us awhile ago so you deserve to die."

"Don't do it!" Curtis shouted.

"We've got to," Benton told him. "Our odds are long enough without adding to them by dragging this scum along."

Longarm's voice turned flat and hard. "Sheriff, I swear that if you kill my prisoner and we somehow manage to get out of this fix, I'll haul you in front of a judge on the charge of murder."

"Custis, you don't—"

"Murder!" Longarm repeated. "Now I know you are hit bad and I know this situation looks hopeless, but don't compound our troubles by executing Weasel. We're *lawmen* and we've taken an oath to uphold the law, not carry it out as we see fit."

Longarm waited, not sure what Benton would do next. The older man's fist was clenching the butt of his pistol so tightly that his knuckles were white. The barrel of his gun was shaking, but there was no doubt that he could drill Weasel through the heart at nearly point-blank range.

Benton finally lowered his gun. "Okay," he breathed, "you win."

"Good," Longarm told the man with relief. "Now let's see if we can cover some ground before daylight. As long as we're alive, we have a fighting chance."

He tied Weasel's hands behind his back despite the man's protests, then prodded him forward. "You know this country better than we do, so find us help."

"I don't—"

Longarm slapped Weasel on the side of his head. The man collapsed, howling like a dying dog. Longarm was ashamed of what he'd just done, but this was a desperate situation and he was sick and tired of hearing the outlaw whine, complain, and tell all manner of self-serving lies.

"On your feet, Weasel! And don't say another lying word. Just lead us to a place that we can hole up in for a while. And if we don't make it, I want you to understand that you will be the very first man to die."

Weasel sobbed and slowly crawled back to his feet. He glared at Longarm with pure hatred and hissed, "You ain't going to make it, Marshal Long, and neither is Benton!"

"Then neither are you," Longarm told the outlaw. "So let's just cut the crap and start moving or by God I will let the sheriff finish you off!"

Weasel staggered forward, walked about twenty yards, and then made a sharp angle to the northeast.

"Where are you taking us?" Longarm demanded.

"There's a cabin."

"Whose cabin?"

"It belongs to a rancher and his wife."

"He means a *rustler*," Benton snapped. "One of his damned cattle-rustlin' relatives, unless I miss my bet."

"We can't afford to be choosy. How far?"

"Ten miles," said Weasel.

Longarm dropped back to support Benton, who looked very shaky. "You heard him. We can be at a cabin by morning."

"And then what?" Benton choked with bitterness. "The Haskill boys will find and kill us anyway."

Custis had no reply. All he could do was his best, and Sheriff Ed Benton needed to do the same. Never give up. Never quit. That was the motto that had seen Custis Long through difficult and dangerous times like these again and again.

Chapter 4

It was a long, hard night of traveling. About midnight, it had begun to rain in a torrential downpour. Sheriff Benton was so weak from the loss of blood that Longarm had no choice but to hoist him onto a hastily made litter. Then he had to untie Weasel and threaten him constantly to make the outlaw help carry Benton across the rough miles. But they were down from the mountain, and Weasel said they were close to the ranch cabin and badly needed shelter. Benton's teeth were chattering and the man was running a high fever. To Longarm's way of thinking, the situation could not have been grimmer.

"I can't carry this damned litter another step!" Weasel cried when he slipped on the muddy slope and dropped his end.

"Pick it up," Longarm ordered.

"No!"

Longarm was grateful for the sheepskin-lined leather coat that had shielded him from the storm. But he was still soaked and in no mood for a debate. So he drew his six-gun, cocked it, and pointed it at the outlaw. "One last time. Pick up the litter."

"I can't!" Weasel showed his teeth. "And I don't believe

that you would kill me either. You're sworn to uphold the law, and that means taking me in for trial."

"So that's your final decision, is it?" Longarm asked, listening to thunder boom over the mountains and feeling the hard rain beating against the rim of his soggy hat.

"That's it, all right. You can't make me—"

Longarm took aim and fired. The slug from his Colt ripped away Weasel's right earlobe and he screamed, grabbing his ear. Longarm's face was drawn and expressionless. He cocked back the hammer of his Colt a second time and said, "Now the other ear."

"Okay, you win! You win!"

"Pick your end up and let's move."

So they slogged on with the light barely strengthening. If anything, the storm seemed to be intensifying, and the wind was getting stronger and stronger, making the pelting rain come at them in sideways sheets. Longarm had the back end of the litter so that he could keep his eye on Weasel and watch where he was going. Longarm was by far the more powerful of the two men, and he could well imagine how Weasel's body must be protesting this awful night.

Time seemed to lose meaning as they pushed on and on. Longarm didn't waste his breath by continuously asking Weasel how much farther it was to the cabin's shelter because he knew that his prisoner wanted to be there too. So he kept his eyes open and his mouth shut.

"There!" Weasel shouted, setting the litter down hard and pointing. "Jethro McCade and his woman live in that valley just up ahead."

Longarm could barely distinguish the canyon's narrow opening through the driving rain. If it had not been pointed out to him, he would likely have missed it even in good weather. It was, he thought, a perfect hideout for a cattle rustler.

"How big is it!" he shouted.

"The cabin?"

34

"No, the valley!"

"Not big. Couple hundred acres of grass, and timber all around the edge."

"How many men are there?"

"Hell, how should I know!" Weasel cried. "I hardly know the ornery sonofabitch! Last time I was here, it was just him and that woman."

Longarm looked around for a good shelter, but saw none, so he said, "Then let's pay them a visit."

Weasel seemed to think that was an excellent idea. For the first time, he grabbed hold of his end of the litter and moved with some alacrity. They stomped through the canyon's mouth and entered the valley with jagged bolts of lightning striking the rim and thunder shaking the ground. Longarm doubted that they were in real immediate danger of being struck by lightning because of the higher trees and rocks all around, but one could never be certain and it was foolhardy to be out in such a furious storm. He peered ahead toward the end of the valley, and it took a while to see the cabin, which rested at the far end of the canyon in a stand of pines.

"To the right!" Longarm bellowed. "Let's take shelter up by the rocks."

"What's wrong with the damned cabin!" Weasel yelled back.

"Do as I say!"

The rocks did offer some shelter, and when they had Sheriff Benton pushed tight under them, Longarm touched the man's cheeks. "Sheriff?"

Benton's lips moved, but he was too weak to be heard over the storm, so Longarm bent close to the man's ear and said, "There's a cabin just up ahead. Once I get things under control there, I'll come back for you. I promise it won't take long. Do you understand?"

Benton nodded.

Longarm edged out from under the rock overhang. "All

right," he said to Weasel, "let's make our acquaintance with McCade."

"He's a mean bastard who will shoot first and ask questions later," Weasel warned, not bothering to hide his fear. "We got to sneak up and take him by surprise!"

Longarm's inclination was to do the opposite of whatever his prisoner suggested, but in this case, Weasel's advice might be sound. "All right then. It's raining hard and we shouldn't have a problem. Let's circle around behind the cabin. And Weasel?"

The tall, dirty man twisted around. "Yeah?"

"I'm going to have the barrel of my six-gun pressed against your spine. Try anything funny and you'll be a dead man."

"I won't. I promise."

Longarm didn't believe the man. "Then let's get this over with."

The rain was coming down so hard Longarm figured they could have just strolled across the valley and stepped up to the front door without being seen or heard by Jethro McCade. Out in the middle of the valley grazed several hundred head of cattle . . . probably all stolen. But it was always better to err on the side of caution, so they spent a bone-chilling half hour sneaking up on the log cabin. A corral full of saddle horses watched them without much interest. The horses looked as miserable as Longarm felt.

"Okay," Longarm whispered when they were finally crouched in hiding against the rear of the cabin. "Now we edge around to the front door. You're going to be in the lead and I'm going to be right behind."

"Don't let me get killed!" Weasel pleaded.

"I'll do my best to see that doesn't happen so long as you don't try anything stupid."

"No, sir."

"Let's go."

They eased around the side of the cabin, smelling smoke coming out of a rusty stovepipe jutting from the roof. There was no doubt that there were people inside, and Longarm thought he could even hear their voices. Instead of front windows, there were rifle portholes, so Longarm and Weasel ducked under them and tiptoed to the door.

"Don't move," Longarm warned as he stepped back, then kicked hard.

The door crashed inward and Longarm shoved Weasel forward. It was dim and smoky inside, but he made out two stark-naked figures humping on a bed. The man on top bellowed in surprise and outrage.

"I'm a United States marshal! Freeze!"

But the man was already reaching for his gun. Longarm tried to step around Weasel, but his prisoner saw an opportunity and grabbed for Longarm's six-gun, which exploded harmlessly into the dirt floor. Weasel bit Longarm on the back of his hand, trying to force him to drop his weapon.

"Shoot him, Jethro!" Weasel cried. "Drill the big bastard!"

Jethro was quick ... too quick. Instead of taking a second and drilling Longarm, his hurried shot struck Weasel in the cheek and blew the man's brains out the back of his head. Longarm felt Weasel shudder in his arms and go limp. Half-blinded by brain and gore, Longarm pulled his gun free. He could feel the cattle rustler's bullets striking Weasel's body, and then one of them knocked the gun in Longarm's hand flying.

Longarm was helpless. Using Weasel as a human shield, he tried to back out to the door, where he figured maybe he could escape, but McCade was advancing, taking his time now with each shot.

All at once the naked woman jumped up from the bed and grabbed a huge, double-barreled shotgun. Longarm tripped over something and fell hard trying to keep Weasel's corpse in front of him. Suddenly he knew that he was going to die, especially when the woman raised the shotgun.

37

Oh, my Lord, he thought, *this isn't how I thought my life would end. Not pinned under a dead man and blown to pieces on a dirt floor.*

That was when the woman pulled both triggers and blew a hole in Jethro McCade big enough for a damned raven to fly through. Longarm watched Jethro leave the ground and slam into the cabin wall, and he also saw the naked woman flying in the other direction as a result of the tremendous recoil of the weapon.

He pitched Weasel's body aside and staggered erect, covered with blood and feeling a painful throb in his hand where Weasel had bitten him and then McCade's bullet had torn away his six-gun. Longarm wiggled his fingers to make sure that they were still functional and that none were missing. Everything seemed to work, so he gazed across the cabin at the woman, who had crashed up against the cabin wall. She seemed stunned, so he went over to her side. "Miss, are you all right?"

She slowly regained consciousness, but when she saw blood on Longarm, her eyes widened in fear and she screamed, then tried to jump up and run away. Longarm held her still. "Miss," he said in a calm voice, "I'm a United States deputy marshal and everything is going to be all right. You saved my life . . . though I don't yet know why. Are you hurt?"

It was a dumb question because the woman had a black eye and puffy lips and had obviously suffered terrible mistreatment. She was in shock, and he knew she needed a little time and attention.

"Here," he said, grabbing a blanket to cover her body. He could not help but notice that she was young with a voluptuous figure. But there were more bruises on her breasts and other parts of her body. "It looks like you've been through Hell and back," he said.

"I . . . I hated him! He took me away from my family and wouldn't let me go back. He used me like an animal!" She covered her face and wept bitter tears.

Longarm put his arm around the girl and held her close until she finally calmed down. "You were abducted and abused, but that is all in the past now. You have nothing more to fear. I'll help take you back to wherever your family lives."

She sniffled. "You'd do that for me?"

"Sure. It's my job, and you saved my life. Jethro had me on the ground with at least another bullet or two, and he'd have killed me for sure if you hadn't opened up on him with that shotgun."

"He's not alone. There's another one that is coming back soon. He's just as bad and he . . ."

The young woman began to shake violently.

"Easy. Easy," Longarm said in a soothing voice. "I can handle this now. You don't need to be afraid of them anymore."

"They'd take turns on me all the time. Just night and day whenever they didn't have anything else to do. I'm probably pregnant! My gawd, what will I tell my parents if I'm with their child!"

She covered her battered face and wept even harder than before. "It's not your fault," he said. "I'll talk to them. They'll understand."

"No they won't! My daddy is a real Bible-thumper and he'll *never* take me back."

"Your ma will talk sense to him."

"She's afraid to argue. I'm lost. I don't have anyplace to go now!"

Longarm felt sorry for the young woman. He didn't know the full story, but he had heard enough to know this girl had suffered terribly at the hands of Jethro and his sidekick. In a way, Longarm was almost hoping that the second man would soon return so that he could be arrested . . . or shot.

"What is your name?"

"Maggie. Maggie Lake."

"Well, Miss Maggie, we need to clean ourselves up now,

and then I have to go back out in the storm and get my friend into this cabin."

Her eyes widened with alarm. "There's someone else!"

"He's the sheriff at Elko and he was shot yesterday up in the mountains. Ed is running a fever and he'll die if we don't get him inside and warmed up by the fire. Do you understand?"

Maggie grabbed his arm. "I know Sheriff Benton! He helped me out once in town and I like him."

"We carried him all night on a litter. He's in rough shape."

"I'm strong enough to hold up my end of a litter."

"Good."

Maggie went to a washstand. She poured water from a skin bag hanging on a railroad spike driven in the log wall, then scrubbed her battered face, arms, and finally her stomach and thighs.

"Here," she said, wetting a dirty towel. "You're also covered with blood. Was it that other fella's?"

"Yeah. His name was Weasel."

"I've seen him before." Maggie looked away from the pair of bodies. "Couldn't we drag them around behind the cabin? I can't bear the sight of either one anymore."

"I'll do that. Dress in something that will shield you from the icy rain."

"Yes, sir."

"Custis," he told her. "Anyone who saves my life has certainly earned the honor of calling me by my first name."

"All right, Custis."

Longarm dragged Weasel and Jethro out of the cabin and around back. A jagged spear of lightning hit a tall tree less than a hundred yards from the cabin, causing it to flame like a pine torch. Thunder boomed across the valley and the rain intensified. He wondered if the man that Maggie feared returning soon was in this valley, or had chosen to take shelter somewhere in the mountains. No matter. When he returned, Longarm would be waiting to either arrest or kill him.

The main question was Sheriff Benton. The lawman had a bullet resting deep in his shoulder, and it would have to be removed or he would die. Longarm had fished bullets out of himself and other men, but it wasn't a job he relished. In fact, he'd rather have taken the kick of a big, Missouri mule. But it was a job that had to be done, and the sooner the better to increase the sheriff's chances of survival.

He wondered if *any* of them would survive given that the Haskill Gang was bound to be looking for them as soon as this terrible storm passed.

Chapter 5

Longarm took Maggie's arm and they hurried out into the ferocious downpour. Even though the young woman had found them rain slickers, the torrent was coming down so hard they were immediately soaked to the skin.

It only took about fifteen minutes to reach the place where he'd left poor Sheriff Benton, but the ordeal seemed longer. Custis bent under the rock and shouted, "We found the cabin and everything is safe now. We're taking you to shelter."

But the lawman didn't offer a reply because he had lost consciousness.

"Is he dead?" Maggie asked, pushing under the rock overhang and staring at the sheriff.

"Not quite," Longarm grimly replied as he reached for the near end of the litter and pulled the sheriff out into the storm. "Let's get him to the cabin!"

Maggie grabbed hold of the litter poles and nodded. "I'm ready."

They started back, and it was tough going all the way. The footing was slick, and they dropped the lawman twice before they finally reached the cabin and set Benton down inside in the middle of the floor.

Maggie pressed the back of her hand on Benton's forehead. "He's on fire," she said, her brow furrowed with concern.

"I know." Longarm peeled off his wet coat. He was shivering with cold, and added wood to the stove. "We've got to dig that bullet out of his shoulder or he won't last another twenty-four hours."

"I don't think *any* of us have long to live," Maggie said. "Johnny could return at any moment."

"Who is he?" Longarm asked as he removed the sheriff's soggy coat, then his shirt, and gently turned the man over to examine his grave shoulder wound.

"Johnny Haskill is no good. He left two days ago to ride over the mountain after whiskey. We expected him back earlier today."

"He might have met Chance and Eli," Longarm told her. "They're the ones that put this bullet in Sheriff Benton and then ran off our horses."

"What are we going to do?" Maggie asked.

"We're going to hope this storm lasts long enough to keep them off our backs. Then we'll see if we can set a trap so that I can either kill or arrest them."

"Arrest them?" she asked in amazement. "You sure don't know that bunch!"

"Maybe not," Longarm answered, "but I'm beginning to understand that they neither ask for nor give any quarter. Maggie, right now we need to try and operate on the sheriff. Heat some water and tear us bandages."

"Out of what?"

"It doesn't matter. Is there any whiskey around?"

"No."

"Then let's get this done before Benton regains consciousness."

Maggie soon had a pot of water steaming on the woodstove. Longarm dipped a rag into the water to wash the blood off his hands and then to clean Benton's shoulder. The bullet hole was dark, festering, and ugly. Longarm knew that his probing would cause the wound to resume bleeding, but that couldn't be helped. "Maggie, if you're weak-stomached, you might want to turn your eyes away."

"If I had a weak stomach, I'd have starved two months ago."

"Is that how long you've been their hostage?"

"Yes."

"I'll try to get you back to Elko as soon as I can." Custis extracted his pocketknife and chose a long, thin blade. "Say a little prayer that I can dig the slug out, or the sheriff is a dead man."

Maggie closed her eyes and whispered a quick prayer. Longarm took a deep breath and made an incision in the already violated flesh. He had to in order to have any chance of extracting the slug. Sheriff Benton groaned but did not regain consciousness, thank heavens. Longarm watched a pool of dark, poisoned blood boil up from the wound as he inserted the blade even deeper.

"Maggie," he whispered, "the slug is even further in than I'd expected. We're going to need a longer blade."

"I'll get you a skinning knife, if that will help."

"It might."

She brought back a long-bladed knife, and Longarm dipped it into the hot water before he gently inserted it into Benton's shoulder. Closing his eyes so that he could concentrate better, Longarm eased his finger into the wound until he felt the ragged edges of the slug.

"Can you—"

"Yes," he said quietly. "Now the trick is to squeeze it between my finger and the knife's blade and gently ease the lead out in one piece. Sometimes even the fragments can cause festering and eventual death."

"You seem to know a lot about bullet wounds."

"I do," Longarm admitted. "Now be quiet because . . . without forceps . . . this is the most difficult, slippery part."

It took a full minute to coax the lead slug out of Sheriff Benton's shoulder, and by then, Longarm's brow was cov-

45

ered with perspiration. But when the twisted metal finally appeared, he relaxed.

"Do you think there are still bullet fragments inside?" Maggie asked, dropping the slug into the pot of hot water.

"I doubt it. Let's rebandage the wound and get him warm and dry. What happens next is out of our hands."

They dressed the wound and pulled Benton close to the warmth of the stove. So close that his soaking wet pants began to steam. Maggie touched the unconscious man's whiskery cheek. "He's really burning up, Custis. I could wet his brow with a cold, wet rag."

"That wouldn't hurt."

"Then that's what I'll do."

The heat suddenly caused Longarm to be drowsy, but he knew that he couldn't afford to drop his defenses. "I doubt that Johnny Haskill is anywhere near this canyon, but we can't be certain, so let's take turns keeping guard," he said.

"You sleep first," she suggested. "You were awake all last night and you need rest."

"Okay," he agreed, getting up and dragging a heavy trunk in front of the door for safety. If Johnny tried to burst inside, Longarm figured he would have enough time to put a slug into the outlaw. "Wake me in an hour or two."

"I will," Maggie promised.

Longarm fell asleep instantly. He slept all the rest of the day as the storm continued to rage. It was dark outside when he awakened to see Maggie still cooling the sheriff's brow with a wet rag. "How is his fever now?"

"About the same, I'm afraid."

"If Ed makes it through tonight his chances are good. Maggie, get some rest."

"I'm all right."

"Just do what I say."

Maggie went over to a corner of the cabin where a few crumpled and dirty blankets were spread on the floor. She smoothed them out and quickly fell asleep. It was obvious that her two captives had treated her like a dog taking the bed for themselves. The young woman hadn't yet recovered, and he knew it was going to take some time before she regained any respect for herself.

The night deepened, but the storm did not diminish its fury. Several times, Longarm heard the sound of a tree being felled by the wind or struck by lightning. No man could travel in this weather, so he went back to bed and slept until late the following morning. When he awoke, Maggie was dressed, her hair was combed, and she was frying bacon, boiling coffee, and making sourdough biscuits.

"It sure smells delicious," he told her after a big yawn.

"Marshal, you're far too thin," she said without preamble. "You've missed way too many meals."

"That's true." He glanced over at Ed Benton. "How's our patient?"

Maggie touched the sheriff's brow. "He still has a high fever, but it hasn't worsened since last night and he's lost no more blood."

"He's tough."

"Yes, but he can't be moved."

"No," Longarm agreed, "he cannot."

Maggie sighed. "Then we are stuck, aren't we? We've horses out in the corral but they're useless."

"If you'd like to make a run for it," Longarm told her, "I sure wouldn't hold it against you. The rain doesn't sound as hard as it was last night. Maybe—"

"No," she interrupted. "I'm not going anywhere without you. Besides, I'm a decent rifle shot and you need my help."

"I expect," he agreed, thinking that it was sad when a girl who'd been through so much already still had to face the possibility of death. "Maggie, how old are you?"

"Eighteen. I look a lot older, though."

"No you don't."

"Yes, I do, and don't try to tell me any different. I feel like I've aged ten years just in the last few weeks." She brushed sudden tears from her eyes. "I'm sorry. The last thing you need is to hear my sad story."

"I'd like to hear it . . . but only if you want to talk."

"There's not much to say." Maggie poured them both steaming mugs of coffee and sat down across from him at the rough pine table. "I was raised in Cheyenne and we had a good life there. My father works for the railroad and he got transferred out to Nevada. I don't like it in Elko and neither does my mother, but we've always done exactly what Father told us to do. And then, I met Johnny Haskill and . . . well, you won't believe this, but I actually fell in love with him."

"Didn't you know what kind of man he was?"

"No. He's a charmer and a smooth talker. He's handsome, and I was just looking for a way out of my house and that railroad town. Johnny convinced me that he wasn't at all like the rest of his outlaw family. He said he wanted to take me far away. We'd go to California and get married. I believed him because I was desperate to escape my father and Elko. Anyway, I sneaked out one night and we took off on horses. When I asked how come we were headed east instead of west toward California, he lied again and told me we were going to Colorado. I thought that was just fine. I would have gone about anyplace with Johnny."

"But instead he brought you here?"

"That's right," she said bitterly. "Jethro and Johnny were best friends, and once they had me here they did whatever they wanted to me. I fought them at first, and I got beaten for my trouble. One would do it to me while the other watched. A couple of times, they both . . ."

Maggie's voice suddenly cracked, and Longarm hurried over to comfort the young woman. "It wasn't your fault."

"Yes, it was! I ran away with Johnny of my own free will. I was stupid and I paid the price. Now, no decent man would have me. I'm fit for nothing but dance halls and back-alley cribs. I'm a whore, Custis! Used up at eighteen and not worthy of being anyone's wife."

"Stop it!" Longarm said roughly. "You're a brave young woman. Everyone makes mistakes. That's how we learn the important lessons of life. What happened here is in the past. I'm not going to tell anyone and neither will Ed Benton, if he lives."

"But everyone in Elko will still know about me and Johnny Haskill! I'll be the laughingstock of the whole town! A scarlet woman. A soiled dove!"

"Then leave town and never return," Longarm suggested, knowing how cruel small towns could be with those who stumbled or committed a social sin. "I'll even put you on the train and you can head east or west, whichever you prefer."

"But I don't know anyone anyplace else!"

Longarm could hear the hysteria rising in her voice. "Tell you what," he decided, "I'll pay your fare to Denver. I've some lady friends that you can look up, and they're good women. Some of them have had bad starts in life . . . just like you have. They'll take you in and help you make a fresh start. How does that sound?"

"Wonderful!" Maggie smiled and wiped away her tears. "Why would you do all that for me?"

"Because you saved my life, and besides, you're a good woman."

Maggie laid her head against his shoulder. "You know something?" she whispered.

"What?"

"After what I've been through, I was hating all men. I hated my father and I hated Johnny and Jethro. I would have killed all three, given half a chance. But then you came here and I realize that I was wrong. There *are* saints in this world."

He chuckled. "Honey, I'm anything but a saint!"

"That's good," Maggie said, voice turning husky. "The real truth is that I'd be disappointed if you weren't all man."

"Girl, I smell bacon burning."

She giggled. "Ooops! I almost forgot. Sit down at the table and let me fill your belly."

Longarm sat and enjoyed a huge breakfast. He ate and ate until he was stuffed, and then he went outside to feed and check on the horses. Each wore a different brand and all of them were quality animals. And while it was still raining, it wasn't as intense, and Longarm had the feeling that this storm was finally going to play itself out in a few more hours.

Maybe we ought to put the sheriff on a travois behind a horse and try to make it to Elko, he thought. *With a little luck, we might even get there in one piece. But the sheriff wouldn't survive the jostling. His wound would reopen and he'd bleed to death before we traveled ten miles.*

Longarm shook his head. He knew that the Haskill Gang would be fidgeting and fussing in their eagerness to find and kill him. The only good thing was that all the tracks would have been washed away in the storm. So the gang might spend days looking before they thought to visit this valley. And by then, maybe Sheriff Benton would be strong enough to help in a gunfight.

"Custis?"

He turned to see Maggie. "Yeah?"

"There's a little hay shed and tack room behind those trees. I didn't know if you would see it, so I thought I'd better show you."

"Point it out and I'll find it."

But Maggie was already walking up a path, and he had no choice but to follow. The hay shed was surprisingly large and well built. There was a pile of cut meadow hay in one corner, while saddles and bridles were neatly stacked along a wall, and there were even several bags of grain for the horses.

"Maggie, I can take care of this myself. Why don't you go inside and stay dry."

"It's dry in here, Custis. And I love the smell of the hay and leather. Besides, feeding the horses is my job."

"Not anymore, it isn't."

Longarm bent to reach for an armload of hay, but Maggie pushed him into the pile, then fell on him, laughing. "You know something?"

"What?"

Her expression turned serious. "I desperately need you to make love to me."

He wasn't sure that he'd heard her correctly. "After all the hell you've suffered with Jethro and Johnny?"

She swallowed hard. "I know it sounds terrible."

"Not terrible, but—"

"Shhh," she breathed. "I can't explain it except that making love to you would be cleansing. It would . . . would erase the sickness of those two men from my mind . . . and my body."

"I don't understand."

"I don't either," Maggie confessed. "But I've thought and thought about it and it's the truth. And I'm afraid that . . . if you refuse me . . . I might not ever want to do it with anyone again."

"Are you sure?"

She began to unbutton her old flannel shirt, and he saw that there was nothing underneath it but a lot of luscious woman. "I'm sure of only this. I saved your life and now you are going to save my belief that at least some men are good and brave and honorable."

"It's the 'honorable' that has me worried right now."

Maggie giggled and pulled off her shirt. "Your turn now."

"This is crazy."

She shimmied her breasts in his face. "I know it is, but some would say *you* would be crazy to deny me what I most need."

He reached out and cupped her breasts in his big hands. "I'm not completely crazy."

She slipped a hand behind his head and drew his face to her nipples. "Show me."

Longarm pulled her close, lips and tongue playing with her breasts as she reached for the buttons of his pants.

"Oh, Custis," she whispered, taking his stiffening manhood in her hand, "you are going to feel so good!"

He wanted to ask if she was sure that this was really what she needed, given the hell she'd just been through, but before he could speak, she was pulling up her dress and guiding him into her slick honey pot.

"Come on, big boy," she begged, "make me forget I've ever had another man!"

Longarm was all too happy to oblige. He moved slowly at first, but she soon became so excited that he threw caution to the wind and began to thrust hard and fast.

"Oh, Custis, you feel so good!"

"So do you," he panted, closing his eyes and feeling a fire building deep down in his belly. He reached underneath her lunging buttocks and pulled her even tighter around himself, grunting, "Come on, girl!"

Maggie began to thrash and shiver. She let out a cry of ecstasy, and then he felt her convulse with powerful spasms. That was all that Longarm needed to unleash his own hot seed deep into her hungry womanhood.

For several minutes, they lay locked together, gently moving to hold on to the sweet feeling. When it finally departed, Longarm rolled off the young woman and said, "Well, do you think we managed to drive out the bad feelings?"

"Yes," she replied. "I feel cleansed and whole again. I feel worthy of being loved by a saint."

That made him chuckle.

"Custis?"

"Yes?"

"Do you think we'll get out of this alive?"

"Of course I do," he told her, turning serious. "I've been in a whole lot worse scrapes."

"What about Sheriff Benton?"

"I don't know," Longarm admitted. "He's lost a lot of blood and he's weak. I'd give him about a fifty-fifty chance of survival . . . if we can stay clear of the Haskill Gang."

"If he dies before they come, couldn't we just run far away?"

Longarm hadn't given the matter any thought, but he did so now a moment before answering. "Sure we could," he told her. "I'd deliver you to safely, then I'd come back and finish what Sheriff Benton and I started."

"But he wouldn't be able to return."

"No," Longarm said, "I'd either have to get help, or else come out here alone."

She hugged his neck. "What if we just went to Denver and you told your boss that the Haskill Gang was too big for one federal marshal to take on by himself? Wouldn't he send a bunch of men?"

"I suppose he would, but he'd want me to return with them."

"But why?"

"Because it's my case and my job to finish."

Maggie frowned. "I wish we were in Denver right now and all this trouble was behind us. I really wish we were someplace . . . almost anyplace else."

A gun cocked with deadly intent. "I'll just bet you do," a strange voice told them from the doorway.

Longarm tried to push Maggie aside, but she held on tight, screaming, "No, Johnny! No, please!"

"Let loose of him, girl! I been a-watchin' you both and now it's *my* turn!"

"Don't kill him! Please don't—"

Johnny's Colt revolver fired, and Longarm felt Maggie's body stiffen even as his own fingers locked on to the butt of his pistol. He rolled hard, raised his gun up, and fired twice. Johnny staggered, and Longarm drilled him again through the chest.

"Maggie!" Longarm cried out.

Her eyes fluttered open and she softly asked, "Didn't Johnny know you can't kill a saint?"

"Maggie, don't die on me," Longarm pleaded as he felt the life gently flow from her body.

Chapter 6

Longarm's mood was as dark as the sky when he buried Maggie in the drizzling rain. He buried her deep and covered her grave with heavy rocks before he pitched Johnny, Jethro, and Weasel into a common, shallow pit. Afterward, he sat in the hay barn and watched the rain continue to fall until darkness. He wished he had a cigar and a glass of whiskey to sort of cap off a farewell to sweet Maggie. Then he remembered her telling him that Johnny had gone away for the specific purpose of getting whiskey.

Longarm knew that the man he'd just killed didn't walk to this valley. So if he could find Johnny's horse, maybe he'd find whiskey. Despite the cold drizzle it was worth a look-see.

"All right," he muttered to himself, "where did he tie his horse? Where would I tie my horse if I was sneaking up on this place?"

Longarm headed into the pines and angled toward the mouth of the canyon. Sure enough, he found Johnny's horse. It was a handsome sorrel mare, and she was upset and wanting to get out of the storm.

"Easy," Longarm said, opening Johnny's saddlebags and finding tins of food as well as three bottles of whiskey and a half dozen big cigars wrapped in oilskin. "Well, at least this is a small silver lining."

He checked the mare's cinch, and found that Johnny had not bothered to loosen it before sneaking up to the cabin. Then, Longarm mounted the mare and rode back to the corral. He unsaddled and put her in the corral along with the other horses. Not a single one of them had the same brand, so he was sure they'd all been stolen.

With Johnny's saddlebags bulging with food, cigars, and whiskey, Longarm trudged through the mud back to the cabin. When he stepped into the open doorway, Sheriff Benton had him lined up in his pistol sights.

"Don't shoot, amigo!"

Benton shakily lowered the gun and stared hollow-eyed at Custis. "I thought I heard gunshots and I figured the Haskill brothers had found us again."

"One of them did."

"What happened?"

Longarm pulled up a chair with Maggie's death still weighing heavily on his mind. He was wet, covered with mud, miserable, and depressed. "We're at an outlaw cabin. I just buried a good woman and three bad men."

"Who was the woman?"

"Her name was Maggie Lake. She told me that she knew you."

"Damn," Benton whispered. "I was hoping she and Johnny Haskill had gone somewhere far away. I even told myself that maybe Johnny Haskill wasn't all bad and he'd turn over a new leaf once he was away from his outlaw family."

"He didn't."

Benton looked around at the tiny interior of the cabin. "This is where he brought Maggie?"

"That's right. Johnny and a man named Jethro McCade were keeping her here as their sex slave. When I arrived, Maggie was in rough shape."

"So they killed her?"

"No, Maggie killed McCade, but Johnny showed up un-expectedly and I managed to kill him . . . thanks to Maggie taking my bullet." Custis ran his fingers through his long, wet hair. "The girl saved my life. I don't know what to tell her family when . . ."

"Never mind her family," Benton snapped with surprising anger. "I'll tell them that she died saving the life of a federal marshal. I have no use for her parents. They never gave Maggie a fair shake, and when Johnny came along and stole her heart . . . well, they just washed their hands of that girl like she was dirt. Can you figure it?"

"No, because their daughter was both brave and beautiful."

"I sure wish I had a smoke," Benton said. "I feel like I'm a hundred years old. I'm as weak as a kitten. When I heard the gunfire, I woke up and tried to get to that rifle that's leaning against the back wall. I failed, but did manage to reach a pistol."

"Ed, I'm sorry to put this to you, but we have to make some tough decisions."

"You mean about the Haskill Gang."

"That's right."

"Fill me in," Benton replied. "How long since I was shot on the mountain?"

"It's been over two days. I had to make you a litter, and Weasel helped me carry you though the storm to this cabin. We're in a little valley that you'd never find unless you knew its exact whereabouts."

"I take it Weasel is dead?"

"He got stupid. Now he's dead."

"Good riddance," Benton said. "So what is the situation right now?"

The storm was bad," Longarm told him. "But at least it wiped out our tracks. I have no idea how long it will be before the rest of the gang comes here. My guess is that they'll be expecting us to make a dash for Elko. But sooner or later, they're going to realize that we tricked them and doubled back this way."

"We've got food?"

Longarm removed the tins from Johnny's water-soaked saddlebags. Next came the bottles of whiskey and cigars. "Ed, we're in pretty good shape. There's enough food here to last us a couple weeks."

"What about horses?"

"We've got a corral full of them . . . all stolen."

Benton almost smiled. "It's still raining out, isn't it?"

"The storm is dying. I figure it will be clearing out in a few more hours. The weather ought to be good tomorrow."

"Then let's have ourselves a couple of drinks and cigars and enjoy life until then," Benton said. "I'm not in any shape to travel yet."

Longarm thought that an excellent idea. He found a couple of cups and filled them to the brim with the whiskey. Next he pried open two sardine cans and handed one to Benton. "Food, whiskey, and cigars. Welcome back among the living, Sheriff!"

They consumed the sardines and washed them down with whiskey. That finished, they lit cigars and refilled their glasses. Longarm stoked the woodstove, and the room grew so warm that they left the front door open and watched the soft rain falling across the hidden valley.

"This would be a hell of a nice place to settle down and raise cattle," Benton finally said. "An honest man could make an honest living here."

"Yeah, but a *dishonest* one could do far better." Longarm smoked a few minutes in silence. "I took a look at the cattle they have here. Pretty big herd. What do you want to do about them?"

"Let's drive them back to Elko. Did you happen to notice what brand they were wearing?"

"Lots of different ones."

"That doesn't surprise me." Benton emptied his glass. He was looking much better, and even had color in his cheeks. "We'll drive the cattle to town and let someone else sort them out. Word will spread and their owners will come in a hurry."

"What about the outlaw problem we didn't get to solve?" Longarm exhaled a cloud of smoke. "I'm not going back to Denver and tell my boss, Billy Vail, that I only got *half* the job done."

"You're a real glutton for punishment, aren't you?"

"I make it my habit to finish what I start," Longarm answered. "And that's what I mean to do with this bunch."

"All right. But give me a few days to rest. Then we'll try to make Elko with the herd and . . . if we don't run into the gang, we'll form a posse and come back after them in force. Once everyone in Elko learns that Maggie Lake was killed by Johnny and sees how many cattle the Haskill Gang has rustled, we'll have a lot of volunteers."

"Sounds good to me."

"Then that's what we'll do." Benton took a deep pull on his whiskey. "What did you think of Maggie? Wasn't she a looker, though?"

Longarm's eyes shuttered and he muttered, "Yeah."

"Why I never saw bigger . . . you-know-whats on any woman. And—"

"Sheriff!"

"Yeah?"

He lowered his voice. "I don't want to talk about Miss Lake. Okay?"

Benton studied Longarm's expression, then dipped his chin in agreement. "You're right. I'm sorry. She saved your life and you hold her in great respect and here I was talking about . . . well, never mind."

Benton raised his cup of whiskey in a solemn toast. "To Miss Maggie Lake, God rest her brave soul."

"To Maggie," Longarm said, turning his head to stare out the door into the drizzling rain.

As Longarm had predicted, the storm blew out by the next morning leaving the sky as blue and cold as glacier ice. Longarm took a rifle and walked out to the mouth of the canyon, being careful to leave no footprints. He sat in the rocks for an hour until he was positive that no one was coming from any direction. Then he moseyed back across the valley, counting stolen cattle and looking at the various brands.

"I tallied just under six hundred head of cattle grazing out there," he told Benton. "And as for the brands, there are so many I lost track."

"Did any one brand stick out?"

"The Rocking A brand was everywhere, and I saw a lot of Diamond Bar cattle."

"That doesn't surprise me," Benton responded. "Those are both large Eastern-owned ranches up to the north. Both operations are run pretty loose. You know how it is when big money from the East buys a ranch and hires someone for straight wages."

"No one minds a business like their own business."

"Exactly." Benton stood up carefully and walked out of the cabin. He was weak and unsteady, but he made it to the corral and back. Slightly out of breath, he said, "I'll be strong enough to travel tomorrow."

"Day after tomorrow maybe," Longarm countered. "I think we're safe here for a while. No sense in taking a chance of you opening that wound before it has more time to heal."

"You trying to coddle me or something?"

"Nope," Longarm said. "The way I see it, we're going to run into the gang and when we do I won't be able to fight 'em off, ride herd all those cattle, and take care of you at the same time."

"Makes sense. If it comes down to it, save the cattle . . . not me."

"I doubt if Miss Louise Martin would appreciate that."

Sheriff Benton's smile faded. "You know something? I've been thinking of retirement. I have some money saved and maybe I could perk up the menu in her cafe. I've even collected some recipes and some Indian dishes that I think would be popular."

"Then give it a try." Longarm took a deep breath of the rain-washed pines. "Life is too short not to do what you most enjoy."

"Well, I've always enjoyed being the sheriff and I've been good at it, but every dog has his day and mine seems to have passed. I almost died on the litter that you and Weasel carried so far. I remember you fellas slipping and then falling a time or two and me rolling into the mud. I had a fever and the rain was ice cold. I had to clench my teeth to keep them from clattering. I was thinking I'd just as soon be dead."

"It wasn't your time."

"Maybe it will be when we try to drive all those stolen cattle back to Elko and run into the Haskill Gang."

"Maybe."

"I wouldn't have too many regrets. I've had a pretty long life . . . especially for a man in my profession. But, Custis, you're still young."

"Younger than you, but not young," he answered. "The thing of it is, I've lived hard and well and I don't fear dying as much as I fear being trapped."

"By a woman?"

"Or in a job I hate. That's why I think you're damned lucky to enjoy cooking so much and to have found a woman who owns a cafe and just happens to be in love with you."

"Hmmm," Ed mused. "I never quite saw it that way. But what you're telling me makes sense."

"Of course it does."

"I saw a buck up behind the corral. Why don't you shoot and butcher him and I'll find some herbal seasonings. We'll spend the next couple of days feasting like kings."

"Okay," Longarm told him. "We got whiskey, cigars, and I'll put some fresh venison on the table. It doesn't get any better than that."

"Yes, it does," Sheriff Benton said. "But this is no time to talk of frisky women."

"No," Longarm replied, "it is not."

He had no trouble shooting a buck that afternoon. The canyon was thick with them, and that night Ed proved himself quite a chef as he used special seasonings he'd found out in the wild.

"If it weren't for the Haskill Gang," Longarm said, patting his distended belly and enjoying his cigar, "I wouldn't mind spending a few extra days here."

"Me neither," Benton said, "but we both know that tomorrow I'll be ready to travel, and we might as well face up to what's left of them thieving bastards. I hate to leave things hanging."

"Me too," Custis said, strolling outside to sip his whiskey, smoke his cigar, and watch for a shooting star. If he saw one, he'd take it as a sign that Maggie Lake was watching over and protecting them. Sure, it was silly, but then when a man was facing long odds, a little silliness never hurt.

Chapter 7

The next morning, Longarm saddled the three best horses and turned the others free. They immediately joined the herd of stolen cattle, and he figured they'd trail along with the herd all the way to Elko. While he was taking care of the outdoor business, Sheriff Benton was loading up all the grub, weapons, ammunition, and bedrolls. They'd decided to tie the works on the third horse as best they could.

"It'd help if we had a damned packsaddle," Benton groused. "But we'll do all right."

"Sure we will," Longarm agreed. "I'm just worried about how you're going to hold up on horseback."

"I'll be fine. You just try to keep the herd moving toward town and I'll take care of myself. Fair enough?"

"Fair enough," Longarm replied.

He helped the older man into the saddle, then gave him the rope to their packhorse, and they were ready to leave. Longarm galloped out to the herd and began pushing them toward the mouth of the hidden canyon. Benton had predicted the cattle would be easy to drive and most likely head for their home ranges, and Longarm found that was exactly what happened.

So far, so good, he thought, keeping a sharp lookout for trouble.

All that afternoon, they pushed the cattle and free-running horses west. That night, they bunched the cattle and made camp about a quarter mile away in some rocks.

"How you holding up?" Longarm asked his friend after getting a small cooking fire started.

"I'll make it," Ed told him. "But I'd rather be rocking on Louise's front porch and sipping a little whiskey."

"At least we have the whiskey," Longarm replied. He frowned, then said, "Sheriff, how are we going to play our cards if we run into the Haskill Gang?"

"I don't know. I can tell you that I'll be in the fight. Don't worry about me not holding my own."

"That's not what I'm worried about," Longarm replied. "I think we ought to have a plan of action."

"We'll fight, what else?" Benton poured them both a cup of whiskey.

"We'll be badly outgunned," Longarm told the man. "My idea is that if we are jumped, we need to find a good place to make a stand."

Benton looked over his cup. "You mean you want to hunker down and let them surround us?"

"No, that's exactly what I *don't* want to happen. If we get caught out on the desert floor, they'll try to catch us in a cross fire. Either that, or shoot our horses and wait us out until we have no moves left except to run for our lives."

"I'm not in much shape to run," Benton said. "So what do you propose?"

"If they jump us, let's drive the herd through them," Longarm said. "Send the whole bunch stampeding into the gang and then we'll try to cut them down in the confusion."

"I like that idea."

They went to sleep early, and didn't awaken until the sun was well off the eastern horizon. Longarm stood up and peered over the rocks, eyes widening with surprise. Down on the flats, the herd was surrounded by what Longarm figured was the Haskill Gang. Several of the outlaws were loping around the cattle in ever-widening circles, and

Longarm felt certain they were trying to pick up his and Ed's tracks. In another ten minutes, they'd be coming in his direction and it wouldn't be to make small talk.

He ducked back down in the rocks and whispered, "Ed, wake up! They found our herd and now they're searching for our hiding place!"

The sheriff jolted out of a heavy sleep. "Huh?"

"We've got big trouble coming our way," Longarm told him. "The Haskill Gang is down below. I'm going to saddle our horses and then we'd better make a run for it."

Longarm started to leave, but the sheriff grabbed his pans leg. "How many?"

"At least a dozen."

Benton sat up quickly. "Damn! Chance and Eli must have another hideout not far away."

"I'm going to get the horses ready. Do you think you can make a race of it?"

"What choice do I have?" Benton asked. "We can't stay here. They'd surround and smoke or starve us out. But I sure hate to run."

"Me too," Longarm told him, "but we wouldn't have a Chinaman's chance against so many. If we can get away, we'll return with a posse and clean this bunch out once and for all."

Longarm slipped around behind the rocks that hid their horses from view. He quickly saddled and bridled both animals, and when he was sure that they were ready to ride, he dropped to his hands and knees and crawled back to his wounded friend. "Let's go!"

Longarm peeked around the rocks just as one of the trackers raised his arm and pointed up in their direction.

"Damn, he's spotted us," Longarm swore. "We're in for it now!"

He hoisted Benton onto his mount and swung into his own saddle. "Let's go!" Longarm shouted as the first bullet ricocheted off one of the big rocks.

They galloped east toward the Great Salt Lake Basin

country. It was a country so vast and inhospitable that you stood a fair chance of dying of thirst in its huge, unforgiving desert. But first, they needed to get over the mountains, and Longarm had no idea of which way to ride without getting trapped in one of the hundreds of box canyons.

They raced stirrup to stirrup with bullets whining in their ears. "We'll be okay once we reach the trees!" Longarm yelled. "Hang on!"

But just then, Benton shouted as his horse fell, pitching him into rocks.

Longarm reined his horse around and started back to help the man, but Benton shouted, "No, save yourself. Go on! Run for it!"

The hell with that, Longarm thought. *Maybe this is as good a place as any to make a stand.*

But it wasn't a good place because there was very little cover.

"Turn around! Go back!" Benton yelled, firing at the oncoming outlaws.

Longarm reached the man and tried to swing him up, but it was impossible. So he bailed off his stampeding animal and sent it rushing up into the trees with a slap on the rump.

"You're a gawdamn fool!" Benton cursed. "You could have made it, and now we're *both* going to die!"

"Nobody lives forever," Longarm said, dropping to a couch and drawing his pistol. He emptied a saddle, but took a bullet crease across his arm. "Sheriff, get down!"

Benton didn't seem to hear him. The sheriff was blinking like a bat and firing as fast as he could pull the trigger. Before Longarm could pull him down behind cover, a slug tore into Benton's chest, knocking him flat.

"Sheriff!"

"I'm a goner. Run for it, Custis! If you make it back to Elko, tell Louise . . ."

The man suddenly choked and then died. Longarm turned to face his enemies. Taking careful aim, he shot the lead rider, and when the man's frightened horse charged past, Longarm mounted the riderless animal and rode hard with bullets swarming around him like hornets. His horse was shot just as he was about to reach cover. Longarm kicked free of his stirrups and landed upright and running for his life. When he finally reached cover, he angled suddenly to the right.

"Where'd he go!" one of the gang shouted in frustration.

"I don't know! Fan out! He can't get far on foot."

Longarm could hear them shouting and crashing through the heavy underbrush. He kept running until he was out of wind, and then he collapsed behind a dead log. Gasping and fighting for breath, he reloaded with the sounds of the pursuing horsemen growing closer. *Maybe,* he thought, *if I can get one of them to come close, I could jump him and take his horse.*

But when Longarm eased his head upward, he could see that the Haskill Gang had fanned out in a solid line. *I haven't got a prayer of hiding here and expecting them to overlook me.*

The line was advancing steadily. Longarm eased back from his log, turned, and ran away, keeping low. If he could get a half mile ahead of the outlaws, maybe he could figure a way to save his bacon. Longarm ran until he could run no more, and then he bent at the waist panting hard. Blood dripped steadily from the crease across his forearm and soaked down from his ribs into his pants.

If they spot me again, they'll run me down for sure. They know this country and I don't. They've got horses, rifles, and water. I've got to keep moving upward because, if they get the high ground on me, it is all over.

He could hear the outlaw gang coming, but they were farther back, and that gave him some hope. Last time he'd looked, the summit was maybe a mile ahead, but he'd have to cross a couple hundred yards of barren, exposed terrain to reach it.

I'll worry about that when I get there . . . if I get there.

Longarm reached the timberline feeling his leg muscles beginning to cramp. He was so winded he couldn't catch his breath, and when he looked back, he saw that the gap between himself and the gang was dangerously thin. So thin that he doubted he had any chance of making it across the barren mountaintop and over the crest. They'd all see him and open fire. At that point, if there was even one marksman in the gang, Longarm would be a dead man.

So what am I going to do? he raged at himself. *If I stay here, they'll find me. I'll be able to kill a few of them, but they'll finish me for certain. On the other hand, if I make a headlong dash for the summit, I'm an easy target.*

Unable to go up or down, Longarm started moving along the edge of the timberline. He would follow it as long as possible and look for an opportunity to present itself. What he needed was a change of luck. Ed Benton's luck had finally run out; had *his* as well?

He could hear the gang cursing and shouting as the hours passed. Whenever he felt his spirits begin to flag like his body, Longarm remembered Sheriff Benton, who had finally decided to exchange his sheriff's badge for a cook's apron and the love of a good woman.

If I'm lucky enough to survive, Longarm thought, *not only am I coming back to settle the score, but I'm going to tell Miss Louise Martin that Ed had decided to ask for her hand in marriage. That's exactly what I'll do. And I'll find Ed's bones and bury them deep and properly.*

"I see him!" one of the trackers shouted, his voice echoing up and down the deep mountain canyons. "He's over there by them rocks!"

Longarm turned to hurry on as a fusillade of bullets peppered the trees and rocks around him. Five minutes later and with the gang closing on his backtrail, he reached the edge of a deep canyon, and the only way down was to attempt the impossible. It was about an eight-hundred-foot drop, nearly vertical, with only a few scrawny trees and shrubs jutting out from the side.

Longarm searched desperately for a game trail or path down into the canyon, but saw nothing. He had about twenty bullets in his cartridge belt, and while that was more than the men he faced, he knew that they were too clever to simply charge forward. Instead, they'd pin him down on three sides with only the cliff at his back, and then they'd wait him out, knowing a man couldn't last very long up here without water.

That would be their best bet. The smart thing to do. So what was the smart thing for *him* to do?

"We've got him trapped!" a man shouted. "Let's flush the bastard out!"

Longarm knew that he had no choice but to descend into the canyon, so he pushed off and began sledding on his backside while attempting to restrain his speed by digging in with his boot heels. It was no use. In moments, he was bouncing down the cliff's steep slope totally out of control. He struck a scrub pine, grunted with pain, and then somersaulted crazily until he was launched off a boulder into the sky. After that, he lost consciousness.

Chapter 8

Longarm did not regain consciousness until just before daybreak. And then he lay immersed in such pain that it was impossible to focus on his situation or surroundings. Gradually, however, as the sun begin to peek over the edge of the canyon, he realized that he lay almost completely buried in a rock slide. Only his head and a foot protruded from the loose but heavy blanket of rock that had swept him almost to the bottom of the canyon.

Longarm struggled to free his arms from the oppressive weight, and then he felt the slide begin to move. With agonizing slowness, he felt himself sinking under the rock, and he struggled frantically to keep from being buried alive. He shouted, but his voice was muffled by the ominous grinding of tons of shifting shale. His nostrils, eyes, and mouth were filled with dust, and Longarm began to choke. Perhaps he lost consciousness again, for when he opened his eyes, he realized that he was almost completely buried.

Longarm breathed deeply and attempted to remember exactly where he was and what had happened to reduce him to this desperate state. But he could not remember anything. Not his name, his calling, or this place. Everything was a blank, and pain dominated his thoughts. It took several minutes to beat back his rising panic, and then his fingers began to do their rescue work as he freed himself from his oppressive grave. The sun lifted higher, and he did not hear a sound other than his own labored breathing.

It was mid-morning when Longarm finally extricated himself from the shifting quagmire of shale. He lay gasping in pain, feeling as if every bone in his body were crushed and he'd been skinned alive. His coat, shirt, and pants had all been torn away, as had most of his underclothes. His boots, however, were still on his feet, and had probably saved them from being broken. One of his knees was badly swollen, as was an ankle. Several of his ribs were broken, but he realized it was almost a miracle that his spine had not been crushed or broken, leaving him paralyzed and completely helpless. His cartridge belt was still wrapped around his waist, but his gun and holster had been ripped away. When Longarm touched his battered face, he felt a mask of dried blood.

What happened to me? Where am I? Who am I? How can I survive?

These questions echoed over and over in his uncomprehending mind, but soon were replaced by an instinctive need to locate food, water, and shelter. Because of his ankle and knee, it was impossible to stand, so he began to drag himself down to the streambed. He could see grass shading its smooth, glistening sand, and wondered if perhaps a small underground watercourse flowed just under its surface. Longarm had a raging thirst. He thought that if he could find water, then he might yet survive.

It took him over an hour to reach the bottom of the deep canyon, and then he immediately set to digging. He did not have to go far until the hole slowly filled with water. Longarm scooped more handfuls of sand and rock until he had formed a generous basin, and then he buried his face in the cool groundwater with a groan of blessed relief. He drank slowly, and when he could drink no more, he cupped his hands and began to wash his face and body. It took a long time to do this, and when he saw how badly his flesh had been violated by the rock slide, he cussed in helpless anger, then lay back and stared up at the silent blue sky.

Where am I? Which way can I go for help?

His gaze examined the rock slide in hopes of seeing a gun or something useful that it had robbed from him, but he saw nothing. Then he focused on the rim, and he wondered if he could possibly have fallen such a great distance. And why had he been up there alone in the first place? Longarm closed his eyes and struggled to remember. But the effort only brought waves of pain and sickness.

Maybe I'll remember later . . . if I can figure out how to survive.

The only thing he understood was that he had no choice but to follow this streambed. Water was life in the desert, and he was certain this lonely canyon fed into high desert because it was filled with yucca, pinyon, and juniper pine. Longarm began to crawl. Every hour, he dug a small well from which to drink. Once, he failed to reach water and he nearly panicked, but then reason returned and he moved only a few yards to the side and again was able to drink.

As soon as the sun slipped over the western rim of the deep, narrow canyon, the temperature dropped fast and Longarm shivered with cold. It occurred to him that the sand underneath was warmer than the air, so he excavated a shallow trench and then covered himself and slept. Longarm awoke feeling light-headed, but his ankle felt much improved. He was able to stand and hobble so long as he kept most of his weight off his twisted knee.

He finally emerged from the canyon at sunset and hesitated, unsure which way to go next. To his dismay, he discovered that the underground water had disappeared. Suddenly thirsty, he retreated back into the canyon and dug frantically until he again found water, but now at an exhausting depth of three feet.

If I leave this canyon, I will lose this underground water and probably die of thirst in one or two days. But if I remain here, I will weaken and eventually die of hunger. So which is the worst of these two fates?

Longarm fell asleep pondering that grim dilemma, and when he awoke the following morning, he realized that he could not afford to drag himself out into an arid, empty wasteland. Far better to remain here and attempt to fashion little nooses or traps out of yucca fibers. If he could snare a rabbit or rodent, or kill some kind of lizard or snake— anything edible to keep up his strength—then his body would heal and he would be able to stand and walk. If he could walk, then he could cover some real ground and his chances of survival would be dramatically improved. Longarm had no doubt that somewhere out in this wilderness, there were human beings who could help him. On the other hand, if he were in Apache country, they might kill him. Either way, he would take his chances.

He did not know or remember how to make an animal snare, but he did see decaying yucca and its strong, pale fibers. It was easy to braid them into a long strand and then fashion a self-tightening noose. So he spend the day making these traps and placing them around the mouth of the canyon. In the early evening, he saw a band of wild mustangs out on the desert floor. They were beautiful, and he longed to possess one and train it for riding.

On his way back into the canyon he was nearly bitten by a huge rattlesnake that lay coiled in his path. Recoiling an instant before its deadly strike, Longarm grabbed a heavy rock. He hurled the missile with all his· strength, crushing the serpent's head. It writhed and flopped about for several minutes, fangs biting. Longarm pounded its ugly head into pulp, then grasped its warm, firm body and lifted it before his mouth. Fighting a queasy stomach, he closed his eyes, then forced himself to sink his teeth into the serpent's body. The meat was warm but he could not swallow the skin, and spat it out. When only the head and tail remained uneaten, he tossed the bloody mess into the brush and crawled back to his precious water hole and slept.

He caught a jackrabbit the next morning. It had choked itself to death in its desperate attempt to be free of his yucca noose. Longarm grinned, splitting his lips. Then he used the edge of a sharp rock to butcher the animal, all the while longing for matches to build a little cooking fire. He even considered trying to start a fire by rubbing two sticks together, but discarded the idea as a waste of time. The only wood available was the remnants of old mesquite bushes, and they were not nearly large or solid enough to stand up to that kind of hard friction. So he ate as much raw rabbit as he could stomach, then rested again, eyes always on the desert before him in hopes of seeing another human being.

That night Longarm again blanketed himself with warm sand and slept. When he awakened at dawn, he checked his traps, but they were empty. He tested his twisted knee, and decided that it was about time to make an attempt to walk until he found help.

But in which direction? If I go the wrong way, I won't have the strength to backtrack. East or west? Which is best?

Tall and slender, almost naked, and covered with scabs and ugly black bruises, Longarm drank all the water that his belly would hold, and then he turned his face eastward, into the warm, rising sun, and began to hobble.

Chapter 9

Longarm was dying of thirst. He had been following a large band of mustangs all that afternoon in the desperate hope that the wild horses would eventually lead him to a desert water hole. But it had to happen soon. Almost naked and badly bruised from his head to his toes, Longarm appeared more dead than alive as he hobbled slowly across the desert.

The mustang stallion, a handsome blue roan, was aware of Longarm's presence, and he kept his band of mares moving, never allowing the man to approach any closer than four hundred yards. Often during that day, the roan would gallop to the rear of his band, lay back his ears, and toss his head at the ghostly apparition that dogged their tracks. But Longarm paid the stallion no attention because it was all that he could do to keep his feet moving.

Water. Over and over he had visions of finding a cool lake where he could bathe and drink his fill. *Water.* His mouth was hanging open and his tongue was swelling to fill his mouth.

The stallion had never seen a man on foot before. Always in the past, men had chased him and his mares on horses, often relaying them so that only the strongest and cleverest of his band were able to escape. But this man was slow and deliberate. As sundown approached, the blue roan felt his own need for water, and finally turned toward the nearby hills and a watering hole less than two miles distant.

It was well after sundown when Longarm collapsed beside the water hole. The blue roan and his band of mares had already drunk their fill, muddying the water. But Longarm did not care as he immersed his head in the shallow pool and drank until his belly was distended and he could drink no more. Then he slid into the pool and sighed with relief as the soothing water eased his pains. Much later, he dragged himself out of the water and lay shivering violently as he gazed up at the stars.

Longarm realized that he was at the very limits of his physical endurance. If he became sick and feverish this night, he would be too weak to move tomorrow and, even with water, might perish.

"Who are you?" a voice asked from the darkness.

"I don't know," he replied, believing the voice was a figment of his imagination.

"You are in very bad shape."

"I am dying and I need your help," Longarm whispered, realizing that he was speaking to an Indian boy and a handsome woman.

"Are you a mustang killer?"

"No. I am . . . I can't remember who I am."

"Ta'oie, build a fire," the woman ordered, laying a thick woolen blanket over Longarm. "We will see if this man is yet strong enough to live."

The boy was smallish and limped badly with a stiff lower right leg, yet he moved well and soon had a fire crackling near the edge of the water hole. Longarm stared at the flames and felt the warmth on his face. Soon, he ceased shivering and his eyelids grew heavy with the need for sleep.

When he awoke the next morning, Longarm felt weak but his mind was clear. He studied the young woman and her Indian companion for several moments, then asked, "Who are you?"

"My name is Keana." She glanced at her Indian friend, who appeared to be in his early teens. "This is Ta'oie. Who are you?"

"I don't know," he told her, knowing how foolish this sounded. "I was hurt somehow and remember almost nothing."

"Tell me what you *do* remember." The woman spoke good English, and now he realized she was at least part white.

"I remember . . . falling." He took a deep breath. "And I remember gunfire. Lots of it. Other than that, I remember only what has happened in the last few days."

"Where do you come from?"

"I walked out of a canyon. Maybe I *fell* into it. In fact, I think I *did* fall into the canyon!"

"What do you want us to do with you?"

"I don't know. Where are we?"

"In Nevada, just south of the Ruby Mountains."

"What is the name of the nearest town?"

"Elko," she replied. "Have you heard of that place?"

He closed his eyes for a moment and concentrated. "Yes, I'm sure that I have."

"Is that your home?"

"Perhaps."

She was squatting on her lean haunches, and he saw that her hair was long and black, fixed in a single thick braid. She was dressed in a faded brown canvas coat, Levi's, and a man's shirt, and he could see that she was tall and slender. Ta'oie also wore white man's clothes, but instead of boots, his feet were clad in moccasins and leather leggings that reached to his knees. They were both wearing holsters, with pistols and large hunting knives.

"You have no clothes," she told him. "But I have things you can wear."

"I could never fit into your size clothes."

79

"Then you can wear that blanket." She frowned. "You have a gunbelt. Where is your gun?"

"Maybe where I fell."

Keana glanced aside at her Indian companion. "Today we will find this canyon and maybe his gun." She looked back at Longarm. "Do you remember your name?"

"No."

She shook her head. "This is bad. We will take you to the canyon and maybe find out these things. Can you ride a horse?"

"I expect so. But my ribs are broken and . . ."

"We will eat, then go to the canyon."

"But how can you find it?"

"Tracks are easy to read."

They had cold beans and tortillas for breakfast. Ta'oie brought three horses and two worn saddles. Longarm had to be helped into his saddle, and then they began to follow his tracks toward the mountains.

"What do you do out here?" Longarm asked the woman later that same morning.

"I catch, tame, and sell mustangs . . . but only to ride, not for slaughter." She motioned to the strange Indian youth. "An army doctor told me that they can fix his leg back East. Take lots of money, though."

"You must mean they could fix him with some kind of brace."

"I don't know that word."

"It's like . . . like a sleeve. It goes around you tight and . . . well, I expect it would straighten his ankle. I don't know, but they might even have to break the bones and reset them properly."

"Yes, that is what he said. You see, Paiutes are foot people. They hunt rabbits, deer, and gather pinyon nuts on foot. They do everything on foot. Not like some Indians who always ride horses. Ta'oie cannot run, so he is very sad and has no friends. All his people laugh."

"Is that why you mustang?"

"How much money do you think doctors cost?" she asked him point-blank.

"I have no idea." Longarm studied the young man. "How did this trouble happen?"

She shrugged. "I think he was stepped on when a baby." "Some say Ta'oie was born that way because he is possessed by evil spirits." Her dark eyes flashed. "This is *not* true!"

The boy gazed up at Longarm. He was small and thin, maybe only four and a half feet tall, with huge eyes and a wide grin. It was obvious that he doted on Keana and that she had taught him proper English. "Mister," he said, "I have only one good friend . . . Keana. She will help me be tall like you someday!"

"I'm sure she will."

"We better go now," Keana said, leading Longarm's mustang up beside a rock and motioning that he should mount the stout little horse.

He did this with some pain and difficulty, for although his ankle was much better, his twisted knee was still swollen and giving him fits.

"We'll ride slow," Keana promised, swinging gracefully onto her own mustang pony and leading the way out of camp.

What had taken Longarm almost two agonizing days to traverse took them less than four hours on horseback.

"This is the canyon," Keana announced at midday. She dismounted and went to inspect the camp where he had set his rabbit traps.

Longarm remembered this canyon and nodded.

"Here!" the woman said. "You killed and ate a rattlesnake! A rabbit too! Look!"

She lifted the snake's head in one hand and a bit of rabbit skin in the other for him to see. Ta'oie pointed out the little hole where Longarm had to dig almost a yard deep for water.

"And you set traps made of yucca," Keana told him,

waving a small noose before his eyes. "You were clever for knowing nothing."

He gazed into the canyon and felt his chest tighten. It was as if there was something very evil waiting for him inside its shadowy recesses. They remounted and started up the canyon. Longarm noticed that both the woman and boy had drawn their carbines from saddle scabbards and were warily eyeing the canyon rim. Nothing was said, however, until they came to the end and faced an immense rock slide.

Longarm examined it, and remembered now how he had awakened nearly buried in shale. "That's my hat sticking out of the rock up there," he told them after a long silence. "I fell down that mountainside. I know it is hard to believe that I could have lived after such a fall, but I did somehow."

"What were you doing on top?" Keana asked.

"I have no idea. I remember waking up and feeling buried alive, but nothing before that moment."

She motioned to Ta'oie, who dismounted. He gave her his rifle, but kept his holstered pistol. With a smile at Keana, he began to scale the steep cliff despite his pronounced lameness. Avoiding the rock slide, he sought out narrow crevasses and outcroppings, and seemed to leap from one to the next as he moved ever higher.

"He climbs like a mountain goat," Longarm said in amazement. "I'd have thought, with his bad leg . . ."

"Ta'oie is strong." Despite that pronouncement, Longarm saw the anxiety in her expression. "Maybe he will find big trouble up there. Maybe you need to shout for him to come back down right now."

"I honestly don't know what he will find," Longarm said, suddenly worried about the boy's safety. "But I wish that he would have stayed here with us."

In reply, Keana dismounted, jacked a shell into her rifle, and pointed the weapon toward the rim. Longarm realized that she was preparing to open fire at the slightest movement or indication of danger.

Ta'oie finally scaled the cliff and disappeared. Longarm

dismounted, grabbed the boy's rifle, and also pointed it toward the rim. And then waited for what seemed like a very long time before the boy appeared. He waved down at them and jumped off the edge as if it were no feat at all. Longarm held his breath as Ta'oie, swinging his bad leg like a small pointing stick, steadily made his way down the cliff face.

"He's remarkable," Longarm said with admiration. "Why wouldn't his Paiute people want him?"

"He can't chase rabbits or run far on a hunt."

"You already told me that."

"Then you are starting to remember better. Huh?"

"I guess I am at that."

When Ta'oie rejoined them, he was clutching a fistful of spent shells in one small hand. "Big shooting up there," he informed them.

"Maybe hunters," Longarm said.

"*You* hunted," Ta'oie told him. "Many men. Blood on rocks. Some died, I think."

"Haskills?" Keana asked.

Ta'oie shrugged his thin shoulders.

Keana walked off a short distance to be alone for a few moments.

"Haskills?" Longarm whispered to himself, finding that the word caused a knot in his stomach. "Who are they?"

Ta'oie shook his head as if the subject were too bad for words. Longarm went over to the young woman. "Look," he said, "I must have come down from there after being trapped by enemies."

"They tried to kill you," she replied. "But why?"

"I don't know."

Keana shrugged. "I hope you remember soon."

"Me too. Are they also your enemies?"

"Until now . . . they left me alone." Before Longarm could respond, she went over to the boy and they conferred in whispers. After a few minutes, Keana returned and said, "Ta'oie saw buzzards circling in the sky that way."

Longarm followed her pointing finger to the east. "I think

83

I had better go and find out who or what died."

"We'll go together," she told him. "But we'll go in darkness to hide from enemies."

"When?"

She studied him up and down. "Two days rest first."

"No. I must find out quickly."

"Then we'll go tonight," she said after a moment, then swung back on her mustang pony and started riding toward the mouth of the canyon.

"Ta'oie?" Longarm said.

The boy had been about to mount his pony, but now he hesitated.

"What kind of men are the Haskills?"

"Very bad. Kill everything they want."

"You mean people too?"

"Kill Indians. Kill mustangs. Kill white people. Maybe you should run away."

Longarm frowned. "If I ran now, I would might never remember who or what I am."

"You are alive."

The boy's meaning was clear and he would say no more, but climbed onto his pony and went galloping after Keana.

Chapter 10

They arose just after midnight and rode to where the buzzards had been seen the previous afternoon. Then, they rested until daybreak with Keana and Ta'oie both keeping watch from high vantage points to make sure that they were not riding into a trap.

"Well?" Longarm asked impatiently when Keana returned to their camp. "Any sign of life?"

"No, only of death." She looked up at the gathering of buzzards. "Maybe just a dead cow."

"Maybe," Longarm said, feeling otherwise. "Let's go find out."

They rode about three miles further and then halted, gazing up at an outcropping of rock where the buzzards were feasting. They could not see what had died because the huge, ugly birds were so thick.

Keana and the Paiute boy dismounted, but when they started up the rise toward the rocks, Longarm commanded them to halt. He was trembling, and his heart beat like a hammer in his chest as he passed the two saying, "I'll do this."

The buzzards were so busy feeding that they weren't aware of his presence until he was almost in their midst. Longarm grabbed a rock and hurled it at one of the hideous creatures, stunning it and causing the others to soar upward squawking in angry protest. He stared at the corpse, feeling his flesh prickle. The man's face was unrecognizable and his clothes had been torn apart by the carrion birds. But Longarm saw something that made him gasp. His hand was shaking like that of an old, old man with the palsy when he plucked the sheriff's badge from what remained of the corpse and stared at it.

Longarm reeled back against the rocks and fought for breath. The stench of death and the buzzards filled his nostrils and made him choke. He turned around and staggered back down to the horses. When the buzzards began to descend to finish their work, Longarm tore Keana's carbine from her saddle scabbard and levered in a shell. He would have emptied it at the birds if the woman had not jumped off her pony and cried, "No!"

Longarm went crazy. He shouted something unintelligible as Keana grabbed the rifle. He tried to tear the rifle away from her grasp, but Keana held on tightly. He jerked her completely off the ground, but she would not let loose.

"If you shoot, they may hear us and come running!" the woman cried. "If you kill those birds, more will come and it will mean nothing!"

"I think I knew that sheriff!" he cried. "He was a good man!"

Keana held her rifle tight between them. "So you are beginning to remember now. Who was he?"

"I don't recall his name," Longarm said, releasing Keana's carbine and showing her the badge. "But he was your sheriff."

"Benton," Ta'oie said. "His name was Sheriff Benton."

Keana looked up from the badge. "Were you with him when he was killed?"

"I . . . I believe so. Who did this?"

"The same ones that made you jump off the cliff. The same ones that left you in that canyon for dead."

"The Haskill Gang?"

She nodded. "So who are you?"

The badge slipped from his fingers and he closed his eyes, hearing the vultures fighting over Benton's flesh again. "I . . . I can't stand them!"

Longarm hobbled up the hill, yelling curses at the buzzards, picking up rocks and hurling them at the death birds until they burst into the sky, raging right back. It took all of his willpower not to turn and run at the sight and the stench of Benton's remains, but Longarm forced himself to cover the corpse with a huge pile of rocks. It wasn't much of a grave, but it was better than nothing.

Pale and shaken, he hobbled back down to Keana and the boy. "Let's go!"

"Where?" She asked. "To Elko? That is where the sheriff came from."

"No. I want to find that gang and kill them one by one."

The pair exchanged worried glances; then Keana reined her horse to the south and Ta'oie followed. Longarm sat watching them for several minutes before he made up his mind to follow.

They rode south for two days, then cut eastward into some high country that Longarm quickly realized was a mustang stronghold. He saw hundreds of the wild animals, and noted that many were of excellent conformation, though all were a bit smaller than a man as large as himself would have preferred. When he mentioned this fact to Keana, she said, "They are descendents of the Spanish horses that were brought over by the conquistadors long, long ago. They were small horses too, but very strong and possessing great stamina."

"I prefer a mount of sixteen hands and over a thousand pounds," he replied. "These mustang ponies are less than fifteen hands and can't weigh more than eight . . . maybe eight-fifty."

"Yes, but have you found your pony to be lacking in strength or willingness?" Ta'oie abruptly asked.

"No," Longarm admitted.

"Then you should not complain," Keana told him. "These horses were born and raised in this rough country. Fancy horses, like those bred to race, would not stand up to this land very long. They would quickly go lame . . . or starve."

"Where are we going?"

"You will see."

Longarm asked a few more times about their destination, but neither Keana nor the boy would give him an answer. So he rode on with them into increasingly wilder and more beautiful country where it was not unusual to sight one or two new bands of mustangs every day.

"I would think this would make fine cattle country and I'm surprised not to see many ranches," he said.

"No lakes or rivers," she told him. "Not enough water for farming or ranching. Otherwise, the mustangs would all be killed or captured."

"Couldn't wells be dug?"

"The water is too far down," she told him. "Only enough water for wild animals and the Paiute people."

"Well," he said, twisting around in the saddle and taking in the vast panorama, "it's a huge, empty land. I just hope that it never sees a gold or silver strike, because that would bring in the people, water or not."

Keana said nothing, but he could tell his words had given her cause to worry. So he added, "I'm sure that this isn't good mining country. But then who would have thought there were fortunes to be made in the Comstock Lode country?"

Keana did not answer but rode on ahead, leaving him to follow.

That afternoon, they reached a Paiute village. It was small, no more that a dozen huts made of sticks and brush. The inhabitants, who probably did not number more than thirty, greeted Keana and Ta'oie warmly, but were very reserved toward Longarm. Their sturdy mustang ponies were penned in a corral made of sharp sticks upon which tumbleweeds were impaled to form what appeared to be an impenetrable wall, but which was really quite flimsy.

"Ta'oie," Longarm asked when they were seated beneath a brush ramada, "are these people your family?"

"All Paiute people are my family," he replied, watching the village children run and play. "Not these anymore than others."

"I meant, do your mother and father or sisters and brothers live among this particular group?"

"No."

Ta'oie did not seem inclined to discuss his family, so Longarm dropped the subject. He stretched out on the ground and watched the villagers go about their daily routine. The women were grinding pine nuts into meal on stone metates, and the children were playing a game using sticks and a ball that looked to be made of horsehide. He did not see many men, and supposed they were off hunting. There were a few friendly dogs in the village, and one, a medium-sized fellow with brown scruffy hair and half his tail missing, seemed to have taken a liking to their tall, battered visitor. He lay down by Longarm's side, and soon they were both dozing away the quiet afternoon.

In the evening, the men of the village returned. They looked at Longarm, but did not greet him. They were short, sturdy fellows who wore a strange assortment of primitive clothing made of rabbit skins as well as more modern shirts and pants. A few even wore various parts of army uniforms, and Longarm wondered if they had ambushed and killed soldiers sometime in the past.

When he mentioned his thoughts to Keana, she shook her head. "Paiutes avoid whites. The only time there was trouble was when the gold seekers going to California and the Comstock came through their lands and cut down their pinyon pines for firewood. Pinyon nuts are their main food. Emigrants would also kill all the deer. But now that the gold fever is past, the whites do not come into this land much."

"That doesn't explain the army uniforms and some of the rifles that I see these men using." ·

"Shoshoni," she explained. "They have always fought white people. Killed some soldiers too. Shoshoni and Paiutes are friends. They often trade."

"I see. Are there Shoshoni in this part of the country?"

"Some. Maybe we will see them. They ride horses."

"And how," he continued, "do these people survive? Surely not on pine nuts and rabbits alone, or they all would soon be eaten."

"Paiutes live like . . . how do you say the word for people who are always moving?"

"Nomads?"

"Yes, nomads. They have small villages like this near water springs and never stay too long in one place."

"I see. Do they help you capture the wild mustangs?"

Keana nodded. "They help me. I help them. I buy things that they need with some of the money from selling mustangs. I save some of the money for Ta'oie, for a doctor to fix his leg."

"You are a very generous woman with a good heart," he told her. "There are not many that would live the way that you do. How did you come to be here?"

"As a young girl, I was traveling to Oregon with my parents in a small wagon train. The Shoshoni attacked because we had killed too many of their deer. I don't remember because I was so small. I ran away into the brush to hide."

Longarm saw tears fill her eyes, and he felt ashamed of his question. "Keana, you don't have to tell me anything more. It's really none of my business."

But she wasn't listening. "I remember being alone for many days and hiding in bushes beside a very bad-tasting river. Now I know it is called the Humboldt. Anyway, I ate frogs and little fish . . . even grass, like horses. The river water made me sick and I grew very weak . . . like you."

"Wouldn't another wagon train have passed by and found you?"

"It was the end of the warm season. Snow was falling and it was very cold." She shivered and wrapped her arms around herself like a little girl, her eyes now bleak and fixed in the distance. "Paiutes found and saved me. They treated me good, like one of their own children."

"But there must have come a time when you met other white people and they wanted to take you back with them."

"No. The Paiutes kept me away from white people until I was tall. By then, I knew that I did not want to live with whites and that I would always follow these people and the mustangs. And there is Ta'oie. I help him like these people once helped me. If not, well, he would never run."

"Keana," Longarm said, choosing his words carefully, "even if he does get to see a good bone doctor or surgeon, that doesn't mean that his leg can be fixed."

Her eyes flashed. "The doctor said Ta'oie will run on a straight leg if it is fixed in the East."

Longarm decided this was not the time or place to try and explain that, contrary to her obvious belief, white doctors could not work miracles. Several times when the boy had removed his thick leather leggings, Longarm had had the opportunity to see Ta'oie's leg—it was a mess. The child's ankle had been broken in at least two places and never properly set. The bones had knitted together imperfectly so that there was a great protrusion that pushed out at the straining flesh. It was a terrible-looking ankle, and might very well be beyond the scope of even the finest surgeon to repair.

"So," Keana was saying, "do you remember anything more?"

"No."

She gave him the sheriff's badge. "You keep this, and maybe it will have some power to bring back memories of your past."

"I'm not so sure that would be such a good idea."

When she looked at him with a question in her dark eyes, he added, "I fear there is much killing and bloodshed in my past."

"Maybe even the great war in the East?"

"Maybe."

"You have many scars of battle. I wonder about your name."

"So do I."

"Would you like me to give you an Indian name?"

"Sure, why not?"

"I'll call you . . . One Who Mostly Forgets."

He smiled. "That's quite a mouthful. Can't you give me a little shorter handle?"

"Lanota." She smiled. "That will be your name among the Paiute."

"What does it mean?"

Keana covered her lovely face and giggled into her hands. "I cannot tell you now."

"Why not?"

"I . . . I would not . . . now."

He shook his head. "All right, but you've really gotten me curious. I mean, a fella at least ought to know what his *own* name stands for."

"You sure you want to know?" she asked, appearing to blush.

"Of course. I won't be offended."

Keana leaned forward and touched his crotch. "It means 'one who has big donkey dick.' "

For a moment, Longarm just stared at her in disbelief and utter amazement; then he threw back his head and laughed so loudly that everyone in the village turned to stare. He laughed until his stomach hurt, and then he wiped the tears from his eyes and said, "That's what you *really* want to call me?"

"Yes, because it is true."

"But . . . but what about all these other people?"

She shrugged, indicating it did not matter.

"But won't they—"

"We will stay here until you grow strong, and by then, they will know this is your right name."

"Lanota," he whispered, patting his large tool cramped by the tight, hand-me-down pants. "I guess it does fit."

Keana nodded, and he saw that she was blushing again.

Chapter 11

Longarm didn't know what to expect living in the humble little Paiute village. He knew that it was a very different life from the one he'd always lived, but he couldn't remember enough of his past to know *how* different. What he did know for certain was that he was in poor shape with a set of broken ribs, a bum knee, and a badly twisted ankle. He also knew that he was covered with scabs and would have appeared a terrible fright to townspeople. But out here somewhere in the wilderness of northeastern Nevada among Paiutes, no one paid him any mind after their initial curiosity had been satisfied.

For the first week of his stay in the village, he did nothing but sleep, rest, and try to rebuild his stamina and endurance by taking increasingly longer walks into the hills. Often, he saw mustangs, wild burros, and mule deer. He even joined a rabbit hunt staged by the Paiutes one morning. They all formed a very long line and slowly beat the brush, advancing and closing in on their terrified quarry until the rabbits were caught in a very small circle. Then there was a great deal of laughter and excitement when the women and children rushed in and brained the rabbits with rocks and heavy sticks.

Most days, Keana and Ta'oie would leave in the morning

and ride out to spend the day scouting various bands of mustangs. At the end of the first week, Longarm asked the young woman about her plans.

"We have a long-standing catch pen about five miles from this village," she told him. "It feeds into a canyon where we corral the mustangs. What Ta'oie and I are doing is scouting out which band we want to capture next."

"What happens once that's decided?"

"Wild stallions lay claim to their own ground and they will protect it to the death. If the band we choose does not have its territory near where we have our catch pen, then we'll have to move everything and rebuild a new trap."

"A lot of work."

"But worth it," Keana told him. "Would you help us?"

"Me?"

"It would be appreciated . . . but do what you want. Come or go away. There are no holds on you."

"I know that," Longarm said. "And when I figure out exactly what I need to do next, I will be on my way. But I don't want to go off half-cocked and make another bad mistake."

"How do you know you made a mistake?"

"I wound up almost being killed. Sheriff Benton *was* killed, and I expect I had something to do with his death."

"I hope not," Keana replied. "Tomorrow, Ta'oie and I will be leaving for a few days. You can come along, if you feel strong enough."

"I'm getting a little restless here. I appreciate the rest and food, but I'd like to earn my keep. I'll go with you. Where are we heading?"

"That way," she said, pointing to the north. "There is a chestnut stallion that I have been thinking about for a long time. He is a fine horse and has sired many handsome colts and fillies. He rules over about twenty mares."

"Which you'd like to steal?"

"Some . . . but never all," Keana answered. "A stallion

needs to keep busy or he loses his fire, huh, Lanota?"

Longarm blushed and then they both laughed.

They left early the next morning leading a packhorse carrying a pick, shovel, wire, and enough food to last them a week. Longarm was feeling better each day, and his only real concern was that he could not remember what role he might have played in the death of Sheriff Benton. Sometimes, he tried so hard to remember that his head ached and he was filled with discouragement. It seemed that his best course of action was just to rebuild his physical strength and hope that his memory would return sooner rather than later.

"Keana, how long have you been mustanging?"

"Quite a few years."

"It couldn't be that many because you are not that old."

"Maybe I am older than you think," she told him.

"You can't be more than twenty-five."

"I'm twenty-six," she replied. "Lanota, how old are you?"

"I can't exactly remember. But there's little doubt in my mind that I'm older than twenty-six." Longarm surveyed the empty land. "How old can a stallion live out in this rugged country?"

Keana considered his question carefully before she answered. "A mustang stallion, if it is lucky, will live to be eight or nine. It might even be strong enough to fight off a rival and keep its band until that age. But after that . . . some younger animal would steal his mares by either killing him or driving him away. I've seen some of those stallions who are too old to defend their herds, and they are usually badly scarred and crippled. Most of them are loners just waiting to die."

"That sounds grim."

"Life is hard," Keana said almost matter-of-factly. "There is little mercy asked for—or given—in this country. When I catch and tame a mustang to be a saddle horse, I try to remind myself that I am giving the animal many extra years of life."

"Yes, but at the cost of his freedom," Longarm reminded her.

His remark caused Keana to look into his eyes. "I agree that is a problem, and it's one that I have often considered, especially since I would not trade my own freedom for a few additional years of life."

"So then . . ."

"So then," she said, "it comes down to this. If I did not capture and sell mustangs, then others would eventually trap the same horses and send them east for pet food. Have you ever seen how cruelly they are treated by men?"

"No."

"If you had, then you would understand. Many mustangs are run to death in the chase and there are those who believe that, if they nick a horse right at the base of its neck with a rifle slug, it will drop and be temporarily stunned. So they do that too, and almost always kill the animal by severing its spine or simply hitting it in the body so that it bleeds to death."

"Listen," Longarm said, "I wasn't judging you or Ta'oie. I was just curious about how you can love wild horses and then live with taking away their freedom."

"Ta'oie and I can live with it because we are kind to them and turn those that will not make saddle horses free again. Those that are either too small or have some conformation problems that would make them undesirable. Do you know how mustangers bring their catch into the stockyards where they are loaded on trains and sent east to the slaughterhouses?"

Longarm shook his head.

"I have seen them with their nostrils wired shut," Keana said with a tremble in her voice. "Because, with their nostrils closed, they cannot breathe well enough to run very far. And others cut their leg tendons or—"

"Enough!" Longarm shook his head. "Look, I understand. Okay?"

"Okay," she replied, riding on ahead with the boy.

At midday, they came upon a good-sized watering hole and rested for several hours. As they prepared to leave, Longarm asked, "Are we in that chestnut stallion's territory yet?"

"I believe so," Keana replied. "And now we will have to be very careful or we will scare him and his band away. Ta'oie, circle around to the west, and we will ride to the east and learn their habits, then meet you back at the last water hole two days from now. Take food and watch for trouble."

The young Paiute spent only a few minutes packing his saddlebags with provisions before leaving them. When he was out of sight, Custis asked, "What kind of trouble?"

"Man trouble. Ta'oie has been shot at before and he understands that white men are not to be trusted."

"Why would they shoot an unarmed Indian boy?"

"For the same reason they kill wild horses . . . because they envy anything that is truly free." Keana's expression was hard and unforgiving. "You should know that I do not trust most white people."

"Does that include me?"

She studied him with her dark eyes. "I don't think so, but you are still a mystery to me and to yourself. Therefore, I cannot be sure of your heart."

Before Longarm could respond, Keana pushed her mount into an easy gallop. Longarm hurried after her, wanting to assure the strange and beautiful woman that he would not betray her friendship, but unable to. They did not speak until late that afternoon when they made camp beside a small stream.

"I'll gather firewood," he offered.

"That will not be necessary. Smoke would warn the mustangs of our presence. They may be very close now." She pointed to a small peak about three miles to the north. "Be-

99

fore the sun rises tomorrow morning, we will leave our horses tied in cover and hike up there to have a good look around."

"We have to go on foot?"

"It is best that way." She raised an eyebrow in question. "Lanota, are you too weak to walk even that far?"

Longarm wasn't sure how far he was up to walking, but he felt he was being tested, so he answered, "I can walk that far and back."

"Good."

They ate a cold dinner, and the moment the sun slipped below the western horizon, it became chilly. Longarm huddled in his blankets and gazed up at the stars, again wondering about his past and future. He doubted he'd remain for long in this country, and was confident that his memory would soon return . . . but was a bit anxious about how he would feel when he did learn of his past.

"Keana, are you still awake?"

"Yes."

"Do you ever wonder what it would be like to live like other white women?"

"Sometimes. But when I have gone to Elko to trade or deliver ponies, I see them and they do not look so happy despite their houses and all their fine possessions. And I have heard their husbands curse them in front of others so that their faces turn red with shame."

"I'm sure you have, but there are plenty of good white husbands."

"Lanota, how would you know this if you don't remember?"

He had to smile in the darkness at her clever response. "I just have a feeling that there are good white husbands, that's all."

"Do you think you have a woman waiting someplace?"

Longarm frowned. "No."

"But you know women."

He rolled over to study her in the cold moonlight. "What does that mean?"

"It means I think that you have slept with many white women. Maybe Indian women too."

He sat up in his blankets and stared at her silvery silhouette. "How can you say a thing like that?"

"I just have a feeling that white women like you and you like them back. That's all I meant." She had been facing him, but now she rolled away and drew her blankets up tight around her neck. "Enough talk. Go to sleep."

"Okay," he agreed, "but sometimes you do say the strangest things."

He was hoping she'd give him some argument so that they could talk a while longer because he wasn't yet sleepy. Then Keana's breathing changed and he knew that she was sleeping. After a while, Longarm sat up and studied her still form. He did not know if he had made love to a lot of women before or not, but he hoped he had. And yes, he also hoped he would one day have the chance to make love to this woman. But he would never force her to do anything against her will. Keana had saved his life and he would always be in her debt, and protect both her and the boy with his life, if necessary.

I find her attractive. I find I want to climb under her blanket and make love. Is this wrong, given that she has helped me live?

Longarm thought about that question for almost an hour, and finally concluded that it was not wrong, just natural. Several times he reached out toward the sleeping woman and then suddenly drew his hand back.

We will make love, he thought, *but when it happens, it will be when she is ready and trusting. Then, it will be very, very good.*

Chapter 12

"Wake up," she said, nudging him with the toe of her boot. "It is time to walk up to the mountaintop."

Longarm jerked awake and rubbed his eyes. It was still quite dark and he could barely see Keana in the fading starlight. "How are we going to see anything if we start this early? We might step into a hole or drop over the side of an arroyo. What's the hurry?"

"The mustangs will already be moving toward food and water," she told him, slinging a canteen and a pair of binoculars around her neck. "We need to see if we can find where they drink first in the morning."

Without further explanation, the woman headed off into the darkness, forcing Longarm to sway to his feet and stumble after her. Keana walked fast with a long, fluid stride that covered a lot of ground in a hurry. Even when they began to ascend the mountain, she barely slowed her pace.

"Hold up!" he shouted in exasperation as his knee started to throb. "Can't you just slow down a little?"

"No. If you can't keep up, either follow at your own pace or go back to camp and sleep. I have no time for talk."

"Well, dammit, you don't have to be so ornery!"

Keana didn't dignify his angry response with a reply, but continued to march on up the mountainside. It was enough to make Longarm forget his knee and sore ankle and go hobbling after the woman. He overtook her about halfway up, but it cost him his breath, while she was hardly winded despite the extreme exertion.

"You ain't leaving me behind!" he gasped.

Keana laughed, but it was a nice laugh. She even took his hand and squeezed it a moment before saying, "All right. We will go slower now and walk with care not to turn over a rock and send it rolling down the mountain. Mustangs have sharp eyes and even sharper ears."

Longarm suspected that she was just saying that to preserve his pride, but was thankful nonetheless. He didn't let go of her hand either as they labored up the rest of the mountain, finally coming to rest in a pile of rocks that offered excellent concealment. The sun was beginning to tinge the dark eastern horizon with a faint salmon-colored glow. And since Longarm doubted he'd ever been in the habit of hiking up mountains just to see mustangs and a sunrise, he sat quietly and enjoyed the view.

First there was a soft pinkish glow on the curve of the earth. Then the glow seeped toward them and he detected the first shadowy silhouettes of mountains, pines, and rocks. Then sunlight began to quickly wash across the immense horizon, transforming it from indigo to a delicious salmon streaked with wispy blue clouds. And finally, the sun burst over the horizon and bathed the barren landscape in the brilliance of liquid gold.

Longarm liked the sunlight warming his face. He closed his eyes, smiled with contentment, and breathed deeply, tasting pine and sage.

She reached out and touched the sleeve of his shirt. "Lanota, despite all your complaints, is this not a good time of day to be alive?"

"It is," he agreed.

Longarm opened his eyes and admired how the gentleness of sunrise made her skin glow, and he felt compelled to lean forward and kiss her mouth. It was a soft kiss, tender and sweet.

"Why did you just do that?" she asked, looking at him with genuine surprise.

"I don't know." He shrugged his broad shoulders. "I guess the world looked so beautiful, and then I turned and I saw in you even more beauty. I simply reacted by kissing you."

He reached for Keana, wanting more of her lips, but she scooted away.

"That was nice," she told him. "But now we must watch for mustangs. That is what we are here for, remember?"

"It's what *you* are here for," he responded. "I'm just along for the ride."

"Hmmm," she mused, unstrapping her binoculars and canteen. She took a drink, then lifted the binoculars to her eyes. "I will have to keep that in mind."

Longarm watched the woman while the woman watched the land. He noted that she scanned the countryside slowly and with great deliberateness. One thing was certain, she had learned the gift of patience. Finally, he asked, "See anything yet?"

"No."

"Maybe Ta'oie is having better luck at spotting your chestnut stallion and his mares."

"Maybe." Keana continued sweeping the vast landscape back and forth with the binoculars. Finally, she mused aloud, "I think there is a water hole about three miles to the northeast."

"Then you've been up here before?"

"Just once when I saw the chestnut and his band last summer. They were being hunted by the Haskill men. Ta'oie and I were in another canyon when we heard the rifle shots and went to investigate. Two of the stallion's mares were down and thrashing in death. They also tried to shoot the chestnut stallion, but he got away and his band followed."

"Haskill? Is that what you called those men?"

She finally lowered the binoculars and studied him closely. "Does their name bring back a memory?"

He took a deep breath. "Yes. I think so, but I can't quite bring it back to mind."

"It will come in its own time. But those men are murderers and thieves. They kill for money and sport. When they see mustangs, they shoot them just to laugh for they have no interest in breaking them to ride."

"I take it that you've had trouble with the Haskills."

"Ta'oie and I avoid them at all costs. So do the Paiutes. The Haskills and their friends shoot a lone Indian man and rape an unprotected girl or woman."

"Have the Paiutes and Shoshoni ever talked about ridding this country of that bunch?"

"Yes, but they know that it would be a bad fight and they would lose many men. The Haskill people live by their guns and would kill many Indians in a fight to the finish. Because we are already so few, the elders are afraid."

"I see."

"But it will happen one day," Keana vowed, unable to conceal the hatred she felt for her enemies. "And when it does I will ride with the men and kill my share.".

"How many men are there to kill?"

"No one knows for sure because they are scattered all over this country. Sometimes most of them will gather to ride and raid together, but not often. I hear that there are more than twenty but that their numbers rise and fall. But I also heard that some were killed in . . ."

Keana's jaw dropped and she stared at Longarm. "Maybe *you* and Sheriff Benton were the ones that had the bad fight!"

"I don't remember."

"Were you his deputy?"

"Keana, I just don't know. I wish I could, but I can't." Longarm shook his head in frustration. "Dammit, this not being able to recall my past is about to drive me crazy!

What if we come upon these men and they recognize me as the one who was with Benton?"

"They would kill you quicker than you could blink your eye," she warned. "So we must not let them see us."

"I won't—"

"Look," Keana suddenly interrupted, quickly lifting the binoculars. "I think I see mustangs!"

Longarm followed her eyes but didn't see a thing, although that was not surprising. He waited several minutes, and when she lowered the binoculars, he said, "Do you mind if I have a look?"

"No." Keana handed him the glasses. "I counted twenty. Tell me what you see."

"I see nothing."

"Look more to your left where the hills come together. That's where they are and the band is moving toward that canyon."

Now Longarm could see the mustangs. They were all light-colored, or else covered with the pale dust of this land so that they seemed a part of the earth. To make matters worse, the rising sun was almost directly in his eyes, forcing him to squint hard. But there was no missing the stallion because he was considerably larger than the mares. Big-necked and short-coupled—Longarm decided that he was one of the best-looking mustangs he'd ever laid eyes upon.

"Let me look again," she said.

He returned the binoculars and she sat frozen for several minutes. Finally, she lowered the glasses and said, "I now count twenty-three."

"What do we do now?"

"We get our horses and ride closer, but stay hidden," Keana answered. "I want to learn what time of morning they go into the canyon where there must be grass and water and exactly when they leave."

"Are they that regular in their habits?"

"You could set a clock by their movements, like some

people. They will only change when the grass or water is gone."

"Well, once we understand their timing, what happens next?"

"We wait until they leave and then we hide at the canyon opening and let them return. When they do, we spring our trap."

"What if the canyon is open at both ends?"

"Then we build a wall of brush that they cannot see through at the back of the canyon. This prevents their escape because horses do not understand the strength or weakness of a wall. If it looks solid, they believe it is as solid as rock and so they always turn back."

"Yeah, that makes sense."

"Let's go," she said "I want to watch their movement closely after they enter the canyon."

So they hurried back down the mountain to their horses and quickly broke camp. Breakfast consisted of nothing more than a hard strip of dried venison, the same as dinner the night before. But Longarm wasn't complaining because he felt a stir of excitement at the prospect of mustanging. There was something about those animals that made his heart beat faster. And even though they were not as beautiful as many domestic horses, just the fact that they were as wild and free as the wind made them seem special.

Keana led off at a trot and when they had circled the mountain, Longarm stayed close behind, noting how she took great care to approach downwind of where they'd last spotted the chestnut and his band.

"They're inside that canyon," she decided aloud as they dismounted in a thick stand of pines. "Now we can sneak up on the rim and get a better look."

"I'm game, but I'm not sure that my knee is up to the test."

"Then you should stay here with the horses."

"Nope," he decided, "I'm coming with you as far as this knee and ankle will allow."

That seemed to please Keana. She led him up a dry wash and around a lot of deadfall before they finally reached the rim, a distance Longarm judged to be less than a mile from where they'd hidden their own mustangs.

"Look!" she whispered, peering into the canyon below and then turning to face Longarm with a wide smile. "Didn't I tell you that the chestnut sires handsome colts and fillies?"

Longarm had to agree. The band was less than a quarter mile distant and clearly visible as they grazed in a meadow fed by a bubbling mountain spring. Most of the younger horses were chestnuts and bore a striking resemblance to their sire. "They're a handsome family, all right. Kind of sad to break it up, though."

"We won't take all the colts and fillies," Keana assured him. "And besides, too large a band invites problems finding enough feed and water. See that young stallion standing off by himself?"

"Yes."

"He is the oldest son and is ready to claim his own mares."

"What's keeping him from doing it?"

"He still fears and respects his father."

"He's a beautiful animal. Are we going to try and catch him?"

"No because he is already filled with his own thoughts of lust and independence. I would judge him to be nearly four years old. Younger horses are better, and that one will breed good offspring. Anyway, I see other mustangs that we can train to be excellent riding horses."

"Look at that," Longarm said grinning sheepishly. "The chestnut stallion has it in mind to make sure his bloodline lives on right now."

They watched as the powerful chestnut went prancing and dancing up to a sorrel mare who was obviously in heat and wanting to be bred. The pair snorted at each other and the mare squealed, then playfully kicked at the chestnut, who nipped her on the haunches, then laid back his ears, reared up high, and mounted her. Longarm's mouth went a little dry as he watched the stallion's powerful hips drive his immense rod into the mare, who braced herself under her leader's weight and energetic thrusting.

Their vigorous coupling did not last long, but when the stallion spewed his seed into the mare, Longarm heard the animal's groan and saw his great body convulse in an orgasm of intense pleasure.

Keana sighed softly, and Longarm realized his manhood was stiff and his palms were sweaty. He turned to Keana, feeling his own desire, and boldly asked, "What do you think about that?"

She met his eyes. "I think the male receives all the pleasure."

He had to chuckle. "Perhaps that is true with horses or even dogs, but with people it's very different."

"Oh?"

"Yes, between a man and a woman, there can be much pleasure given and received by both."

She studied him, lips parted slightly. "I . . . I very much doubt that. I have heard Indian men and women couple and it is always the man who howls, not the woman."

He reached for her. "Keana, let me show you how both a man and a woman can enjoy coupling more than you could ever imagine."

She scooted away from him for a moment and he did not try to grab her. "I am afraid of it," she said.

"Don't be. I will be gentle. I promise that you will receive far more pleasure than pain."

"I have heard the cries of young girls who have never . . ."

"Keana," he whispered, "you are not a young girl. You're a full-grown woman and you are ready for a man. One who can teach you how a man should make love to a woman."

"Rough like the stallion, I'll bet."

110

"No. Easy and slow. Gentle and loving." He smiled. "Don't be afraid of this thing. Let me show you how good it can be when it is done right."

"I have always wondered about it," she confessed. "Always watched animals couple and tried to find pleasure in the eyes of the female, but could not."

"I will bring you *great* pleasure. I swear it."

Her eyes dropped to his crotch. "I see that your man thing is trying to escape your pants. It wants inside of me."

"Yes, it does," he admitted. "And, if you let me kiss and touch you in the right places, your woman thing will soon beg to hold it deep inside."

She took a ragged breath. "Would you mount me from behind like . . ."

"Maybe later, if that way pleased you. But for the first time, no. Come here."

Keana inched closer until her beautiful face was only inches from his. "Lanota," she whispered, "be good to me."

"I will," he promised, gathering her into his arms and easing her back to the ground. She was a strong young woman, but she offered little resistance as Longarm unbuttoned her shirt and began to lick her hardening nipples. He alternated this with sucking on them until Keana was moaning with pleasure and reaching to unbutton his pants.

"Here," he said, spreading his coat on the ground so that her back would not be scratched or bruised. "I'll help."

"I . . . I honestly haven't done this," she blurted out, looking up at him, her eyes round with fear and wonder.

"You'll want it over and over," he promised, pulling off her boots, socks, and then her pants. As he'd expected of a woman living in this hard country and not accustomed to towns, Keana wasn't wearing any underwear.

"You have a magnificent body," he told her as he removed his own shirt and pants, studying her large, firm breasts, flat stomach, and long shapely legs.

"Your body is good too, but . . ." Her eyes widened in

fear as she stared at his immense rod. "Lanota, maybe you are too much man for Keana!"

"No, I'm not," he replied, tossing the last of his clothing aside and then pressing her flat against the ground. "It might hurt for a moment when I first enter, but then it will soon feel very good."

She reached up and kissed him hard. "I want to believe you, but . . ."

"Keana, it is your time."

He reached down and wiggled his middle finger against the bud of her passion until she began to squirm and moan. Then he inserted his finger into her honey pot and stirred it gently until he felt her hot juices flowing.

"When will you try to enter me?" she panted. "I . . . I think I am ready!"

"I like to take my time," he explained, easing her legs apart and kneeling before her so that his manhood began to nudge and tease her womanhood, causing her to raise her hips in hungry anticipation. "I don't want you to think that every man mounts a woman like that chestnut stallion and then suddenly starts pumping until he is finished."

She closed her eyes, mouth open, tongue flicking, and he pushed his rod a tantalizing inch into her now-hungry body. "You are a virgin," he declared, fighting off an almost over-powering urge to drive himself down into her all at once. "A real mustang maiden. But now I'm going to change you into a mustang woman."

"Oh, yes! Hurry, Lanota, I want you in me all the way!"

"A moment of pain, Keana, then I promise you a long, sweet pleasure."

When he broke her maidenhood, Keana stifled a cry, then raised her knees and grabbed his buttocks, pulling him deep and whispering, "Don't move! Let me feel what this is like and be still."

He raised up on his elbows. "Is the pain passing?"

"It is gone and now I feel a fullness that is very good."

"It's going to get even better in the next few minutes."

"I believe you now, Lanota. Do it to me as you like."

Longarm started slow. His narrow hips moved in an easy circle round and round until he could feel the woman begin to thrust. Her legs came up and she locked her ankles behind his lower back, pulling him into her body.

"Take it easy," he said, watching a smile of pleasure spread across her face. "Go slow and make it last."

"I don't ever want this to end!"

They kissed hard until Keana lost control and she began to buck and thrust with all of her strength. She was a powerful young woman and her legs locked him in a viselike grip.

"Something is coming over me!" she cried. "Something I've never felt before."

"Don't fight it!" he growled, his own body starting to take control of his will.

Suddenly, Keana clawed at his back. Her lips pulled away from her teeth and her eyes flew wide open as she stiffened in orgasm and then shuddered violently, all the while alternately groaning and howling with intense pleasure.

Longarm kept pumping until she went limp. Then he climbed off and raised Keana to her hands and knees. "Now it is the stallion's turn," he hoarsely growled into her ear.

He clasped her hips and began to thrust just as powerfully as the chestnut stallion had only a few minutes earlier down in the canyon. Keana threw her head back and gasped with pleasure while Longarm filled her completely with his spurting seed.

Chapter 13

They finished their lovemaking just in time to watch the chestnut lead his band out of the canyon and turn south. They dressed in an easy silence that lasted until Keana said, "You were right and I should have believed it when you said it is much better between a man and a woman than with animals."

"Yes, if there is pleasure-giving on both sides," Longarm told her. "A selfish man will want to satisfy himself."

"You're the only man I want."

Longarm started to remind her that he was a stranger, even to himself, and that one day he would be leaving Keana and Ta'oie. But when he looked into her eyes, he decided that she already knew this and words weren't necessary. Theirs would be a sad, difficult farewell, and there was no point in even thinking about it. They had mustangs to catch and tame, and that was enough to occupy their thoughts for now.

"Where will the stallion lead his band?" he asked as they walked back to their horses.

"It is of no importance," she told him. "We only need to know when they enter and leave this canyon. Did you see that it is open at both ends?"

"Actually," he confessed, "I was so intent on the mustangs that I forgot to look up the canyon."

"There is a way out there at the top that is hidden behind the rocks from below. The mustangs will know about it and we will have to close it off."

"How wide is the opening?"

She pointed at a distance between two rocks that Longarm estimated at thirty yards. "That's going to be a lot of work," he said.

"Ta'oie and I will help you."

Her remark caught him by surprise, and it must have shown because Keana laughed when he said, "Me?"

"We'll do it together in less than one day and night," she told him. "Starting after they leave this canyon at this same time tomorrow."

"You and that Paiute kid don't sit around wasting much time."

She finished buttoning her shirt and despite what they'd just done together, Longarm had to suppress the urge to taste her breasts again. She saw his interest and smiled. "Lanota, how often does a man want to do that?"

"About as often as he can, and that's pretty often actually."

"I need some time. Could we wait and not do it again until tonight?"

She was quite serious, and he killed a devilish grin to say, "That will be just fine. So what happens now?"

"We wait to meet Ta'oie, make camp and then love, then in the morning we come back here and when they are gone, we close off the escape."

He snapped his fingers. "Just like that, huh?"

"Yes."

Longarm thought that all sounded great, especially the part about making love tonight.

Ta'oie immediately sensed that they had become lovers. The boy didn't say a word, but when the sun went down, he took his blankets and went off to sleep alone. Longarm and Keana took their pleasure again, and afterward he asked, "You don't think that kid is mad or jealous about us doing this, do you?"

"Ta'oie?"

"Who else?"

"Of course not!"

"Well, he didn't look too happy when he went off into the dark a while ago."

She frowned. "Maybe you are right and I should talk to him about this coupling we do now."

"I don't think that is such a good idea. In fact, I think it would be a very *bad* idea."

"You don't know Paiutes."

"And you don't know men."

"He is only a *boy*."

"I think he thinks he's more of a man than a boy," Longarm assured her. "But he's your friend and mustanging partner, so you do what you think is best."

"I will."

Very early the following morning, they rode the same loop back to the canyon rim and hid until the chestnut returned with his band. Longarm noted that the stallion entered the canyon first, snorting and acting spooked as if he were aware of some slight change in his surroundings. The horse even reared a few times, and Longarm swore it looked up at them hiding behind the rocks.

"Keana," he asked, keeping his head down low, "do you think he saw us?"

"I would think not," she replied. "But a stallion that old will have escaped many traps and dangers. He must be smart or he would not survive so long."

"Maybe he caught our scent," the Paiute boy said, speaking for the first time all morning.

"No," Keana told him. "The wind is blowing up the cliff into our faces. But I agree that the stallion senses a hidden danger which is making him unusually cautious. We are fortunate that he will not be able to see our work below until he is well inside the canyon, and by then it will be too late. We will only have one chance to catch him. If we fail, he will drive his family far away and we will never catch sight of him again."

They watched the large band of mustangs drink, graze, and rest for two hours, and then the stallion was ready to leave. He galloped around the band, ears laid back tight, and drove his charges out of the canyon.

Keana and Ta'oie both glanced up at the sun, noting the exact time. When they were certain that the mustangs were at least a mile away, Keana said, "Let's get our horses and start building the barrier. There is no time to waste."

That afternoon, Longarm began to understand how difficult it was to close off the top end of the canyon in order to trap the chestnut stallion's band of mustangs. Thirty yards was a long stretch to fill, and they had to be careful not to leave any evidence of their work that could be seen from the mouth of the canyon, allowing the wary stallion to sense a trap. That meant that the pines they used in their barrier had to be cut up on the canyon's rim, then lowered on a rope.

"Why can't we just toss them over the side?" Longarm asked. "It sure would be quicker."

"Yes, but then the stallion would see where the freshly cut pines struck the walls and dislodged rocks. There would also be the remains of broken branches dotting the cliffs, and these would be like red flags. As it is, we must hope that the wind is blowing up the canyon so that he does not smell the sap from these cut pines."

"I had no idea that trapping mustangs would be this complicated," Longarm grunted, picking up the ax and selecting a pine to fell. "I never considered horses to be that smart."

"They are not especially smart," Keana explained, "but mustangs are very suspicious and can sense danger. With their good eyesight and excellent sense of smell, they are hard to trick. And when you have an older stallion who has outran and outwitted men before, then he becomes doubly difficult to fool."

"I hate to think of all our effort going to waste."

"Sometimes that happens. Ta'oie and I have failed before. But we do better than most because we understand mustangs as few white men do."

"How many animals will you decide to break to the saddle?"

"We won't know until we can watch them closely. There are mustangs who, even at an early age, will never be tamed. They will either fight you to the death or run away at the first chance. Those animals would rather die than lose their natural freedom."

Longarm spat on his palms, grabbed the ax again and started chopping. He worked steadily all afternoon, cutting the pines and then tying them to a long rope and slowly lowering them down the cliff. Ta'oie or Keana would then carry the trees over to a line of shallow postholes they had just dug in the ground. They would set and wire the trees together so that they formed a solid barrier, one that would appear to the mustangs to be too impregnable.

Each time Longarm lowered a felled pine, he studied the progress below and found himself rather proud at being a part of this undertaking. Sure, Keana had warned him that it might fail, but . . . well, they were making a hell of a good try, and it was going to be very interesting to see the results.

At dusk, Keana appeared on the rim. She looked as exhausted as Longarm felt, but said, "We can make love now, if you want."

"Frankly, I'm a little bushed for that," he confessed. "And you don't look any too eager either."

"I'm very tired, but I thought a man had to . . ."

"Naw," Longarm admitted. "A strong young man will generally want to make love every day, but that doesn't mean he can't go without it for quite a spell if he's working too hard or gone off somewhere."

Keana was obviously relieved. "Maybe we can do it to-morrow night."

"Let's just wait and see how we both feel," he told her.

They walked over to the rim and looked down at their nearly finished barrier. Ta'oie was still hard at work. "That kid does a man's work, no question about it," Longarm said. "Even with that lame leg, he'd put most people to shame."

"Ta'oie will not stop until we are finished. He is tireless. Wait until you see him ride the mustangs."

"Will *you* be breaking them as well?"

"Of course. But Ta'oie will ride the worst fighters."

"I'll be content to watch from the sidelines," Longarm told her.

"Can you use a lariat?"

"You mean can I rope a horse?" When she nodded, he said, "I doubt that I was ever a cowboy. I'm probably not that much of a bronc-buster either."

"We don't whip and spur them into submission," she told him. "That is not the way to tame a horse and leave it with some dignity."

"I guess maybe it isn't."

"We only need a couple more trees," she said, heading back down the little mountain goat trail to the canyon floor. "Then come down and help us collect brush and fill in the holes. It is important that the mustangs cannot see through our wall."

He reached for the ax, feeling his blisters burn. "Two more pines coming up."

"No," she said, managing a weary smile, "coming down."

They worked long after sundown, using the starlight to show them where to plug up the holes in their thirty-yard-long barrier. Longarm watched as Keana made a final inspection and tested the wall to see if it would remain stand-ing.

"Keana," he observed, "if a strong wind comes up all of a sudden, it will blow them all down."

"I know, and let us hope that does not happen until after we have roped the ones we want to tame and built them a strong corral."

"Sounds like a lot more work to me."

"But not as hard as what we have just finished," she told him. "But for now, we are finished. In the morning, we will all hide near the mouth of the canyon and wait for the chestnut and his family to arrive."

"Then we spring the trap once they are inside."

"Yes."

That night Longarm and Keana made another cold camp up on the rim almost directly above the opening of the canyon, while Ta'oie sneaked down to be closer to the entrance. When the mustangs passed, he would run out and block their escape, scaring them toward the far end, where they would be stopped by the flimsy wall of pines.

"When they are all trapped inside," Keana said, "we will ride in on our horses and cut out the stallion and the others that we want to turn loose."

"Couldn't that be a problem?"

"Things can and usually do go wrong," she admitted. "The important thing is that none of us get hurt and none of the mustangs are injured. It is necessary to remember that none of this is worth getting killed over."

"I agree," he said, body aching and eyes heavy with the need for sleep. "See you in the morning."

"Sleep well, Lanota."

Longarm gazed up at the stars, and even though he was battered and bone-tired, he found he was also excited and could hardly wait to see what the morning would bring.

Chapter 14

A few stars were still in the predawn sky when they saddled their horses and rode up on the rim. They tied the animals and silently hiked down to the mouth of the canyon, where they hid behind some boulders. As sunlight seeped slowly across the plains to burnish the canyon walls, Longarm suddenly realized that Ta'oie was staring at him in a way that made him uneasy.

"What?" he asked the Paiute kid.

"When do you leave us?"

"I don't know. Why?"

"I do not think you belong here," Ta'oie told him. "Soon you will be well enough to leave and go away."

"Ta'oie!" Keana scolded. "What is the matter with you!"

"He does not care about mustangs. He only wants to breed with you!" The youth's eyes burned with hatred and jealousy. "He goes away soon . . . or I go!"

Keana moved over toward the boy, but Ta'oie recoiled, scooting out of her reach.

"Listen," she said quietly, "Lanota is our friend."

"No friend!"

"We can talk about this later," Keana told him. "The mustangs are coming. They will be here soon and I have to depend on *both* of you."

"I'll go to the other end of canyon," Ta'oie told them defiantly. "Wait for the stallion to come and chase him back. Then we'll see how much help Lanota gives you."

"No!"

But the boy was already on his feet and scampering up the rocks. Keana shouted, "Ta'oie, we need you here with us!"

He looked back down. "Maybe you don't need Ta'oie anymore. Maybe Lanota wants to do something now I don't want to see!"

"Damn," Longarm whispered. "That kid is really jealous and upset. It's all my fault."

"No, it's mine," Keana argued. "I should have had a talk with Ta'oie, but I was too embarrassed. Now, it might be too late to make amends."

"You want me to go after him?"

She shook her head. "You'd never catch Ta'oie. And besides, I was thinking about asking him to go to our back canyon barrier."

"Why?"

"I told you that a horse will never try to run through what it thinks is a solid wall. However, if they stampede and come around that dogleg too fast, they might not be able to stop in time. If that happens, they'll crash into our flimsy tree wall, knock it down, and we'll never see any of them again. Ta'oie can keep that from happening by jumping out in front of them before they reach the dogleg just before the wall."

"But he'll be on foot!"

"He knows what to do," she said, sounding very confident. "Ta'oie understands horses better than anyone except myself. I've taught him well."

Longarm had jumped to his feet when the Paiute boy had gotten upset, but now he crouched back down in the rocks. "Keana, maybe it wasn't my fault but I still feel bad about the kid. I like Ta'oie and thought he liked me."

"He does. That's probably why he is so upset."

"He's smitten with you," Longarm told her. "Didn't you know that?"

"I guess, but I couldn't figure out how to handle it," she replied. "I'm almost old enough to be his mother."

"Well," Longarm told her, "Ta'oie sure doesn't think of you like a mother. I could see that right from the start."

"What am I going to do?"

Keana looked so upset that Longarm edged over and slipped his arm around her slender waist. "I'll be leaving someday and the problem will take care of itself. Until then, I guess we'll just have to be a little more discreet about our lovemaking."

"What about kissing and touching? Are we going to have to pretend that there is nothing between us!"

"Let's have a talk with Ta'oie and explain how it is between a man and a woman. And it might not hurt to again remind him that we're trying to get enough money to have a real good surgeon operate on his ankle so that he can walk upright and proud."

She beamed. "You said 'we're'! Does that mean that you'll help?"

"What do you think I'm doing now?" Longarm smiled. "Don't answer, 'cause right now I'm just causing trouble. But that will change and I will help you get the money for Ta'oie's operation."

Keana hugged his neck, then kissed his lips. "Would you like to make love right here and now?"

"What?"

"We have time before the mustangs come, and who knows when we'll have the next chance? Between having to deal with Ta'oie's jealousy and the mustangs, we're going to be very, very busy the next few weeks."

"Keana, I'm not an excitable man at the crack of dawn."

She unbuttoned her shirt and pulled it back so that he could see her big, perfect breasts. "These excite you, don't they?" she asked, shaking them a little.

Longarm's mouth suddenly went as dry as sand. "They sure do!" he gulped.

Keana unbuttoned her pants, watching his expression closely. "And what about this? Doesn't it also excite you?"

"Oh, hell, yes, it does!"

"Then come make love to me, Lanota. Be my stallion again!"

Making love in the rocks at daybreak wasn't according to plan, but Longarm discovered that his manhood had its own timetable and agenda. So he took the woman into his arms, laid her softly on the dirt, and was soon acting every bit the wild stallion she so loved.

"Lanota!" Keana whispered an hour later. "They're coming!"

They had dressed after their lovemaking, and now Longarm sat up and peered over the rocks. "Yep," he said, "it's the chestnut and his mares, all right."

"Stay down," she urged, grabbing him by the collar and hauling him lower. "And we must be very quiet."

"No conversation?"

"None," she said, demonstrating her seriousness by buttoning her shirt right up to her throat. "I mean it. If they hear us or even think they hear us, they will run away and not return maybe for weeks."

"Be a damn shame to waste all of yesterday's hard work." Longarm studied the blisters on the palms of his hand. "Whatever I was before I lost my memory . . . it sure couldn't have been a miner or lumberjack."

"Shhh!"

They crouched in wait, listening to the stomping of hoof-beats and then the suspicious snorting of the chestnut as it warily approached the mouth of the canyon. Longarm knew that the mustang could not see or hear them, but he suspected that it might smell them, if the wind was blowing down through the canyon.

Keana had rolled onto her back, closing her eyes so that she could concentrate on listening, and Longarm decided

126

to do the same. By placing the tender palms of his hands on the earth, he swore he could feel it tremble under the pounding of hoofbeats.

Finally, Keana rolled over on her side and whispered in his ear. "They are inside the canyon now. Let's sneak down there and keep them from escaping."

"How?"

"With gun and rifle shots," she answered. "They won't charge us if we are firing into the sky."

"Are you sure?"

"Yes!"

"You'd better be . . . or we're mincemeat."

Keana moved quickly down from the rocks to dash out into the canyon. With his swollen knee and sprained ankle, Longarm was slow to reach her, and by then, the stallion and his mares realized they had entered a trap.

"Here they come!" Keana shouted, drawing her pistol and raising it overhead. "Don't shoot until I do!"

Longarm drew his pistol and raised it, feeling the earth shake as the mustangs came galloping down the canyon straight at them.

"Now!" Keana shouted, firing her weapon three times in rapid succession.

Longarm did the same, and the effect of the gunshots was dramatic. The wild horses skidded to a halt behind the stallion, who reversed direction and went flying up the canyon toward the opposite end and what he believed was his last chance for freedom.

"What do we do now!" Longarm yelled.

"You stay here and keep them back! I'll run up on the rim and get our horses."

If she hadn't disappeared so quickly, Longarm would have appreciated knowing what he was supposed to do if the stallion, realizing there was no escape at the top of the canyon, suddenly decided to trample him.

He thought he heard Ta'oie firing rifle shots, and then, only a few moments later, the mustangs appeared. This time, however, the stallion was driving his mares with his teeth.

"Holy cow," Longarm grated, as he quickly replaced his three spent cartridges, "this had better work!"

He waited until the band was about two hundred yards away before he raised his pistol and fired three quick shots. The mares in front broke ranks and spun back into the stallion. Terrified, their colts and fillies went right after them despite the chestnut's efforts to stampede them over Longarm.

Confused and frightened, the band raced back and forth in the canyon until they became exhausted. Then, the mares and young ones dropped their heads and struggled to catch their wind while the indefatigable stallion galloped around and around his band, whinnying with such desperation that the sound cut at Longarm's heart.

It seemed like forever before even the stallion came to a weary halt and watched Longarm and Ta'oie, who had appeared at the canyon's opposite end. *The chestnut knows he's trapped,* Longarm realized, *but he's afraid of our guns because someone has shot at him before. He is scared but he will never surrender.*

"Lanota!"

Longarm turned to see Keana, who shouted, "Mount up, but stay here and I'll try to separate the stallion from his band and then drive toward you. Let him pass outside!"

"Okay!"

"And there will be others I will send your way. Let them go too."

Longarm's saddle horse was so excited it kept dancing around, which made it extremely difficult for him to mount. But he finally managed, and then Keana galloped on toward the band. When it saw her approaching, the stallion issued a shrill challenge. It did this over and over, and it took a while for Longarm to realize that Keana was slowly positioning herself between the leader and his band. Once that was accomplished, she raised her gun and fired just over the chestnut's head.

The stallion bolted in fear and raced past Keana. Its ears were flattened against its head and it came flying down the canyon toward Longarm as if it were a runaway train. The chestnut suddenly veered at Longarm, causing his mount to scramble up into the rocks. It was all that Longarm could do to keep his seat as the stallion raced out of the canyon, but it did not go far. Longarm watched the horse spin and then come prancing back, still determined to save his mares.

"Yahh!" he shouted, firing another bullet into the sky and sending the stallion trotting off some distance.

"Lanota!"

He turned to see both Keana and the Paiute boy riding frantically to overtake the band bearing down at him on the run.

Something had gone very wrong! Keana had told him that she and the boy would separate the band into keepers and those to be released back to the stallion. Longarm forced his mount back into the mouth of the canyon. He tried to raise his gun, but the horse underneath him went crazy and began to buck. Longarm kicked out of his stirrups and landed hard. He staggered painfully to his feet, then calmly began to empty his six-gun, firing six or eight feet over the leaders' heads.

"Back!" he shouted, deciding that he would give them another fifty yards and then he'd attempt to reach cover before their flying hooves cut him to pieces.

At the very last instant, the lead mares shied away, peeling off toward the canyon walls with the rest following until the entire band was milling in circles.

Keana appeared out of a cloud of dust and shouted, "You did it! But this time, let the small groups pass."

A few minutes later, Keana and Ta'oie were sorting the animals they wanted to keep from the others. Longarm didn't have to be told to step aside, and things seemed to go smoothly for the next hour or so until about half of the mustangs were in the canyon and the rest had rejoined the anxious stallion.

"That's it," Keana said, her face and hair powdered with a fine, chalky dust.

"What happened when they *all* came at me!" Longarm demanded. "It wasn't supposed to happen that way, was it?"

She shook her head, expression grim. "Lanota, let *me* talk to Ta'oie about what went wrong."

"I was nearly trampled to death."

"I know, but you stood your ground and turned them back. Ta'oie will have seen your courage."

"I don't give a damn about impressing him!" Longarm snapped. "Do you think he tried to get me killed?"

"No."

"Well," Longarm announced, slapping dust from his clothes, "I'll have a hard time trusting the kid a second time."

"Please. Let me speak to Ta'oie alone."

"All right. What's next?"

"Stay here. Don't let the stallion back into the canyon. Meanwhile, we will rope the mustangs we want to tame for riding horses."

Longarm was angry but he let it pass . . . for now.

They roped and anchored seven young, promising mustangs to the same pines that Longarm had chopped and lowered down the canyon wall the day before. The mustangs tried to run away, but soon realized that they could not get rid of their anchors.

"We'll watch and make sure that they do not get caught in the rocks and strangle or injure themselves. While this happens, they'll become accustomed to our presence and then even start to look forward to our help."

"And that's how it begins?" Longarm asked.

"Yes. We have some grain to entice them. You will see

how quickly they become like pets if they're not mistreated."

Longarm, believed her. And although he was furious at Ta'oie for what he thought was a calculated attempt to get him killed, he had to admire the kid's ability around wild horses and the way that he could ride and handle a lariat. For the first couple of days after they settled into the watching routine, Longarm kept a close eye on Ta'oie, who always avoided looking at him directly.

He's either hating me or he feels guilty, Longarm thought. *I sure hope it's the latter, or we are going to soon have a bad parting of the ways.*

"Keana," he asked one evening when Ta'oie slipped off to sleep apart, "did you question him about what went wrong?"

"Yes, and he said it was not his fault. The horses were scared and acted strangely."

"That's it?"

Keana shrugged. "Ta'oie has never lied to me. I do not think he is doing so now."

"I'm not sure I feel the same way," Longarm told her.

"Give him time, Lanota. Just a little more time. I will talk to him again soon."

"If you don't, I will."

Keana nodded with understanding and went to check on her newly captured wild horses.

Chapter 15

The next few days were anticlimactic and seemed to pass slowly for Longarm. They built a small round corral out of the pine trees they'd already cut, but did little with the seven mustangs.

"Lanota, they are terrified of us right now," Keana explained. "It takes at least a week for them to become accustomed to our presence. This is a time for rest and for patience."

"And then?"

"We will begin handling, haltering, and leading them," she said. "After they get used to that and can stand our touch, we will saddle each animal."

"I expect that is when the action finally begins."

"Some will try to buck the saddle off, and we let them try until they understand that this will not work. A few days later, Ta'oie will climb into the saddle and begin to ride the mustangs."

"That's when they'll really uncork," Longarm said.

"No," she answered. "Ta'oie will not allow that to happen."

"Why not? Is he afraid of taking a hard fall?"

"Of course not! But you see, if a horse is successful in bucking, it will do it again and again. What we try to teach them is to accept the weight of a rider without the *thought* of bucking or rearing."

"Whatever you say," Longarm told her. "You two are the experts. I'm just here to help out."

During the week that followed, Keana and Ta'oie followed the steps that had been outlined to Longarm. At each stage of the training, the mustangs reacted with fear, but by applying their patience and skill, Keana and the Paiute were able to keep the fighting to a minimum. And sure enough, at the end of two weeks, the ponies were all accustomed to being saddled, bridled, and led around.

"It's working just like you said," Longarm told them one evening. "But we'll see what happens tomorrow morning when Ta'oie finally steps into the saddle."

"You will see frightened mustangs that maybe crow-hop around a little but nothing more."

"No bucking?"

Ta'oie said, "I will keep a very short rein so that they cannot get their heads down by their knees. If they cannot put their heads low, they cannot buck."

"Makes sense," Longarm replied. "But I still don't understand why they won't buck later when they have the chance."

"They have no good reason to buck tomorrow . . . or later," Keana told him. "Horses that buck are *fighting* their riders. Ta'oie and I don't give them any reason to fight."

Longarm finished his supper and climbed into his bedroll. As usual, the Paiute kid went off to be by himself and Keana came to Longarm.

"Lanota?" she asked.

"Huh?"

"If you never remember your past, what will you do with your future?"

"I don't know."

"Stay with me and Ta'oie. You are good around horses and we could . . ."

He rolled over on his side and studied her in the moonlight. "Keana, I don't want you to think about us having a future together. I don't know where I came from, but I'm sure that I'll remember sooner or later and go back. This is a good life, but it's not one that I'd want on a permanent basis."

"Why not?"

"I have a feeling that I'd enjoy a cigar and some rye whiskey. That I like doses of city life mixed with the outdoors. I think I know how to play cards, and I'm sure that I must have been a lawman."

"What makes you think so?"

"For starters, I'm good with a gun and I knew Sheriff Benton. I was probably with him when he died, and that means I might have been his deputy."

"He didn't have a deputy, Lanota. I remember that now. And as for being good with a gun, it might only mean that you were a hunter."

"I'm better with a *pistol* than a rifle. Nobody hunts wild game with a pistol. The only thing pistols are good for are hunting and killing men, and I am sure I wasn't a gunfighter or outlaw."

"But what if you were? What if you *are* a wanted man ... an outlaw with a price on his head? If that were the case, then you could find no better place than to be with Ta'oie and myself in this big, empty country."

"Keana ..."

"Listen," she said. "It is possible that there is a bounty on your head. And ... don't be angry with me ... maybe you even killed Benton yourself!"

Longarm sat up and stared at the mustang woman. "That's crazy talk! Don't say anything more about me being a killer. I may not remember yet who or *what* I am, but it isn't a killer."

"No," she said in a subdued voice, "you are not a killer. But there may be men trying to kill you that you don't know about. Is that not plenty of reason to stay hidden for a few years?"

"Years?" he echoed. "I couldn't spend years out here. What do you do when the snows fall?"

"We keep to our wikiups. It is not so bad if you have enough blankets and food to eat. You need only gather wood and keep a fire going to stay warm. I do not mind winter and neither does Ta'oie."

"I would." Longarm yawned. "We've got a big day tomorrow saddling all those mustangs and then watching Ta'oie give them their first riding lesson. So why don't we go to sleep."

"Only if you give some thought to staying out here because you might be a wanted man . . . even a cold-blooded killer!"

Longarm scoffed at the suggestion, but when he didn't go to sleep immediately, he realized that anything regarding his murky past was possible. What if he was wanted for murder or some serious crime that would either send him to prison or a gallows?

You can't be wondering and worrying forever, he reminded himself a few minutes before he went to sleep. *You have to finish up this mustanging business and go find the truth about yourself.*

When he awoke just after sunrise, Keana and Ta'oie were already with the mustangs, talking to them in low, reassuring tones as they were being haltered.

"Need any help?" he called.

"Just watch and learn," Keana replied.

Longarm took that advice to heart. He wished he had a cup of coffee and a cigar, but since he didn't, he made a fire and then burned a slab of salt pork and some old sourdough biscuits. By the time he was finished with breakfast, all the mustangs had been haltered, brushed, and quieted.

Longarm cleaned his plate and fork, then wandered over just in time to watch Ta'oie select a pretty filly to ride. This was the most docile and gentle of the bunch, and when Ta'oie saddled her she barely trembled. Then, without a moment's hesitation, the young Paiute leaped onto the filly's back and sat there as relaxed as if he were reclining on a big sofa.

The filly turned its head around and stared at Ta'oie with one eye as if to ask what he was doing on her back. When the boy reined her head back around and nudged her flanks with his heels, the filly trotted off as nice as you please. Longarm watched in amazement as the pair rode clear out to the canyon's mouth, then returned without a bit of fuss.

"What do you think about that?" Keana asked, hands resting on hips.

"It's pretty remarkable," Longarm confessed. "That horse acts like it has been a kid's pony instead of a wild mustang."

"Yes," Keana agreed. "But what is going on between the filly and Ta'oie is more than meets the eye."

"What does that mean?"

"It means that he has already gained the filly's trust. If Ta'oie were tense or even if he moved too suddenly, she would try to buck. As it is, the filly is not fearful of him now on her back."

"What if I tried to ride her?"

"She would probably buck you off," Keana told him.

"Would the filly try to buck *you* off?"

"No," Keana said, "because we understand each other."

Longarm had no doubt that Keana and Ta'oie knew exactly what they were doing. This was confirmed when Ta'oie saddled and rode every one of the green mustangs. A few of the colts did hump their backs and try to buck, but Ta'oie never gave them enough rein to get their heads down and they didn't seem all that interested in a fight.

That afternoon, Ta'oie gave the mustangs a second riding lesson. This time, he rode each horse completely around the inside perimeter of the canyon.

"Ta'oie," Longarm said, "you have a real gift with horses."

For the first time since Longarm had met Ta'oie, the kid really looked pleased and happy. "Keana has taught me everything about wild horses. How to catch them, yes, but also had to win their respect and love. These are good animals. They won't go to slaughterhouses, but will make good riding horses for a white man and his children."

"What about for a Paiute man and his children?"

"Paiutes like to walk. Feeding a pony takes too much time and work."

"But *you're* a Paiute."

"Ta'oie is a Paiute but also a mustanger . . . like Keana." The kid's eyes dropped to his deformed ankle. "Lanota, you know that Ta'oie does not walk so good anyhow."

"Maybe that will change. The day might come when you will walk as well as any of your people."

To this, Ta'oie just shrugged and said, "I still like to ride mustangs better."

After that, he and Ta'oie were easier around each other, although Custis was sure that the kid still very much preferred him to be entirely out of the picture.

Since there was not a lot for Longarm to do but watch Keana and Ta'oie work with the mustangs, he spent a good deal of his time hiking into the mountains and taking target practice with his six-gun and his rifle. This was a satisfying pastime because he did seem to be a natural with firearms, especially with a pistol. He also enjoyed the feeling of being alone in the wilderness and testing his ability to hike farther and farther until he felt as if he could walk all day and not be especially fatigued.

"Well," he said one morning after both Keana and the Paiute had exercised the mustangs, "when are we heading to Elko to sell this bunch?"

"Soon," Keana replied, not sounding very thrilled with the prospect.

"How much will they bring?"

"After our supplies, not more than a few hundred dollars."

Longarm frowned. "That's a lot less profit than I expected."

"How much would good surgeon cost to fix Ta'oie's ankle so that he can walk straight and run?"

"I have no idea," Longarm told her. "But I'm afraid that it would be considerably more than two hundred dollars."

"Hmm," Keana mused. "Maybe we should go after that gold."

Longarm had been stretched out in the shade on his bedroll, but now he sat up. "Gold? What gold?"

"Big gold mine," she told him, making a vague gesture to the northeast. "Much gold is there, but it is difficult to get."

"Difficult? Why?"

Keana did not answer his question directly. Rather, she posed a question of her own. "Lanota, what if someone stole something from someone, then killed them? Who then would own the thing that was stolen?"

"Don't talk to me in riddles. If you have a question, ask it plainly so that I can understand."

"Maybe I will someday."

Longarm shook his head in exasperation. "You're a puzzling woman. I was about to take a nap, but now I'm wide awake."

"I'm sorry."

"Who stole what?" he demanded five minutes later when his curiosity got the best of him.

"The Haskill Gang killed a prospector who had much gold," Keana replied. "Ta'oie knew that old man well. He was a friend of the Paiute and we gave him a good burial."

"How did he die?"

"He was shot many times."

"How do you know who really murdered him?"

"Ta'oie and I sneaked up close to the old man's gold mine and we saw the Haskill men digging gold. Lanota, who does that claim belong to now?"

"I would expect it belongs to the dead prospector's next of kin."

"He had no family. I know this because he told us once.

Lanota, if we killed the men that shot the prospector, would his gold become *our* gold?"

"I suppose so," Longarm said quietly. "I don't remember exactly how it would work, but I am quite sure that the gold mine would not belong to the gang. In fact, they would be arrested and maybe even hanged."

"But what about the gold that has already been found?" she persisted. "That is what I am talking about."

Longarm steepled his fingers and considered the question from all sides, then said, "If the prospector had no relatives and no last will leaving it to someone else, then it would belong to us."

A big smile lit up Keana's pretty face. "That would be plenty enough money to pay for the operation. Enough money to buy a ranch with a real house . . . if you would stay with us."

"Why don't we just take things one step at a time."

"But what about the gold!"

"In the first place you haven't told me where the mine is, and in the second place I have no idea how many men we'd have to face."

"The mine is less then thirty miles from here," she told him, almost bouncing up and down with excitement. "We could go there tomorrow!"

"What about the mustangs?"

"We'll leave them here for Ta'oie to work with for the next few days. He would like that."

"And what if things went bad for us with the Haskills? What would happen then?"

"Ta'oie would return to his people with these good young mustangs and be considered wealthy."

"Okay, if that's what you want, then we'll go take a look at that gold mine."

"You'll kill the Haskill men and we'll take all the gold."

"Hold on now! There might be too many."

"Then I'll kill some too," she told him. "The Haskill men are very bad. Killing them would be a good thing."

"And you're not the least bit worried about our own hides?"

She shook her head, her eyes now firmly fixed toward the northeast.

Longarm could not help but follow her gaze and wonder exactly what he'd allowed himself to be talked into. *Oh, hell,* he thought, *maybe this is all a figment of her imagination. Or the gang has worked the claim out and gone away. Lots of things could happen other than us getting into a gunfight over a gold mine.*

Lots of things . . . and almost all of them bad.

Chapter 16

As they rode out of the canyon heading toward a gold mine that was probably either worthless or imagined, Longarm twisted around in his saddle and gazed back at Ta'oie, the mustangs, and their little camp and corral. The Paiute was saddling one of the colts in preparation for riding. Longarm waved, but the kid either didn't see him or didn't care to respond.

"Ta'oie sure wasn't concerned about us leaving," Longarm said, turning back around in the saddle and looking at Keana. "And here I thought I'd broken the ice and we were finally becoming friends."

"Think nothing of it. Ta'oie likes and respects you, but it is not their way to make much of a good-bye."

"I thought he'd at least wish *you* good luck. After all, you're the only family he has and the one who has helped him from the start. Why, for all he knows, you could get killed!"

"Ta'oie believes that when it is one's time to die, he will die. He doesn't believe that luck has anything to do with living."

"Don't you believe in luck?"

"No, because it is only a white man's wish. I believe that we get what we create for ourselves. If we are good, good comes to us. If we are bad, then that too will come. People who are sad make their own sadness. Happy people make up their minds to be happy."

"What about bad breaks?"

She looked at him intently. "Such as?"

"Such as Ta'oie getting stepped on when he was little and having his ankle get all messed up."

"He could have been sad and bitter, but that was never his nature. So he worked hard and when I first saw him, I felt the goodness of his being and knew that we would make a team. Ta'oie had to work very hard to overcome what he lacks, but he did and so now he is better off than most of his people. Someday, Ta'oie will become a strong and wise leader among the Paiute. One of the few of his people who understand the white man."

"And white women," Longarm added.

Keana's lips formed a half smile. "I am not like the other white women. I know that, for I have spoken to them in Elko. They care nothing about mustangs or the outdoors. Once, I even went to one of their churches because a good woman told me that I was bound for Hell unless I was baptized."

"Did you get baptized?"

"Sure, why not? It made the woman very happy. She fed me apple pie and gave me a holy Bible . . . even though I told her that I could not read."

"What happened to the Bible?"

"I gave it to another white woman who could read." Keana raised, then dropped her shoulders in a gesture of resignation. "What good is any book if it cannot be read? What good is Jesus to Indians if they have to be baptized before he will help them? None of the Paiutes have been baptized, but they are good people who have their own beliefs. I do not think they will go to Hell, but I do not know about this for sure."

She was looking right at Longarm, and he knew that she wanted a serious reply, but he just shrugged.

"You have nothing to say about these things?" she asked.

"Nope."

"Have you been baptized, Lanota?"

"I have no idea."

"So, if you will burn in Hell if you aren't baptized, will you have it done? It is important because Hell sounds like a very, very bad place. Hotter and drier even than this country, by far."

"Keana," he replied with a hint of exasperation, "you're asking me questions for which I have no answers. We're supposed to be going to a gold mine that was stolen from a murdered prospector. And to get that gold, you tell me we might have to kill a bunch of men."

"Killers themselves," she spat in contempt. "Men much worse than red devils! Lanota, if there is a God and he believes in justice, then he would appreciate us killing them all."

"I'm not sure that is true," Longarm told her, "but I can't say that it's wrong either."

"You don't seem to have much of an idea about God or the devil."

"You're right. But I'll think about them after I remember who and what I am. Right now, I'm just trying to sort out and answer the simple questions. And I don't understand Ta'oie acting so cold when we left, especially toward you."

"He knows I will return if it is meant to be. He also knows that it would do harm to be sad, so he chooses to work with the mustangs and be happy. Is that so hard to understand?"

"No."

"Look," she said, raising her hand and pointing. "It is what you call a dust devil, no?"

"Yes."

The dust devil was only about ten feet tall, just a baby twister merrily dancing through sage, tumbleweeds, and pines. Its spinning, erratic movement brought back to Longarm a memory of his childhood, and he knew that he had once owned and played with a top.

"We will see who can chase it down first and become one with it!" Keana shouted, sending her pony racing ahead.

Longarm sent his mustang pony chasing after Keana, and she would have easily beat him to the dust devil except that it was moving so erratically that it skirted her onrushing horse and came whirling straight at Longarm's mount. His pony shied violently and the next thing Custis knew, he was straddling a big sage bush.

"Damn!" he swore, rolling off and watching Keana go chasing his pony. "This is what I get for acting like a fool kid!"

Keana had a lariat tied to her saddle, and Longarm watched her shake out a loop, then send it sailing over his pony's head. A few minutes later, she came riding back leading his mount and wearing a huge, satisfied grin.

"Don't say a word," he warned, still plucking stickers out of his pants. "Not a word."

Keana burst into laughter, but otherwise kept mum. However, every time he glanced sideways at her that afternoon, she burst into giggles.

We're supposed to be riding into a war with the Haskills and she acts like we are going to a Sunday picnic. I'll never understand this mustang woman.

They made love that night and left early the next morning, heading into ever more desolate and arid country. They had large canteens, and Keana seemed to know all the water holes, but the landscape was so inhospitable that Longarm said, "I guess only a gold-fevered prospector would enter this kind of Hell."

"There are those with other reasons."

"Such as?"

"To escape."

"From the law?"

"Or worse. And there are many wild horses in this country. Ta'oie and I have caught many here."

Longarm stood in his stirrups. They faced an immense sage-choked basin ringed by treeless mountains dotted with volcanic lava. Other than some more dust devils and a few buzzards circling many miles to the west, Longarm swore that there was not a living thing within a hundred miles.

"Keana," he said, "you told me that the prospector's gold mine was only thirty miles, and we must have gone nearly that far already. So where is this mine?"

She pointed to the east. "That low set of mountains has water and several canyons with grass and trees, but you cannot see them from here. The gold mine is in one of the canyons. We should stop now and rest, then ride up to the mine tonight."

"I can't imagine anything out here, but I'll take your word for it." Longarm dismounted. He watched Keana loosen her pony's cinch, and did the same. She led her horse over to some rocks, and after making sure that there were no rattlesnakes, tied the animal. She removed her hat, then her shirt to reveal those golden breasts that he had been enjoying.

"We'll sleep until dark now," she told him.

"Fine, but taking off your shirt doesn't make it any easier."

Her eyes dropped to his pants. Then she said, "You need me now?"

"Maybe later," he replied. "How many outlaws do you think are working the gold mine?"

"Only four or five the last time Ta'oie and I were here to watch." Keana closed her eyes. "You can shoot them all, if you want."

"That's not as easy as you might think."

"Then I will help. Either way, we will kill them and take the prospector's gold to pay for Ta'oie's surgery. Okay?"

Longarm nodded, but wasn't comfortable with the notion

of gunning down men without giving them a chance to surrender.

It was dark when they awakened. They did not make love, but instead resaddled their horses and rode silently across the top of the basin. It was a raw, windy night, so Longarm pulled a bandana up around his face and kept his head down low. He let his pony follow Keana's mount while his mind drifted deeper into his shadowy past. Suddenly, it came to him that he *had* been a lawman, but not Sheriff Benton's deputy. What then? A federal marshal?

Yes!

Longarm's head snapped up and as he clearly recalled he had been a United States marshal on assignment to capture a band of Nevada outlaws. He had come from someplace distant . . . perhaps Denver or Santa Fe.

Don't force it, he told himself. *Remembering everything will happen in its own time. Be patient! But now you know that you're a sworn officer of the law and are therefore bound by oath to give these outlaws a chance to surrender. Yes, but what if they refuse and there are enough of them to get the upper hand? Can you afford to take that chance with Keana's life?*

"Lanota?"

Longarm was torn abruptly from his troubled reverie, and realized that Keana was tying her horse in a thicket of pinyon pines. He looked about with more than a little confusion. "Have we already crossed the basin?"

"Just the top part." Keana stood beside his mount. "You were lost in thought, but now we are close to the prospector's gold mine."

He dismounted, tied his horse, and began to loosen his cinch, but Keana said, "Better not do that in case we have to run."

"Good idea." Longarm grabbed his rifle. "Lead the way."

She turned and started off on foot. The wind was still gusting and when Longarm glanced up, he saw ghostlike clouds scudding fearfully across the face of a frigid moon.

"How far do we have to walk?" he hissed.

"Not far."

Longarm concentrated on his footing because the path was littered with stones and it would be easy to twist and badly reinjure his knee or ankle. They moved single file through more pinyon and juniper, and then Keana abruptly came to a halt. "There is where they sleep tonight."

It took Longarm a few seconds to recognize the dim outline of a mining shack, then a corral and horses. "Where is the gold mine?"

"To the left of the shack where a tunnel goes back into that hill about fifty paces."

"I count four horses," Longarm told her.

"There are five," she said.

"All right, five. But that doesn't mean there aren't more men than that inside the shack."

"Or less. I will steal their horses. That way, if there are too many and the fight goes bad, they cannot catch and kill us."

"You can't handle five horses by yourself. I'll help."

"I will steal only two at a time. Stay here and kill them if they hear me and rush outside."

Her plan made sense. He needed to stay back and cover her retreat if the plan went sour. "Just . . . just be careful."

"If they come outside you better shoot straight and fast, Lanota."

"I will."

Keana kissed his lips, then headed directly toward the corral. Knowing horses were spooky at night when rushed, she took her sweet time; Longarm had to admire her steady nerves as she almost strolled toward the corral, speaking softly to the now-attentive horses. Keana disappeared for a moment in shadow, but when she reappeared, Longarm saw that she had located bridles. A few minutes later, she led the first pair away after securing the gate. She brought the animals to where he was hiding, and handed him their reins, saying, "Tie them back in the trees while I bring two more."

"All right, but be careful."

Longarm wasted no time in securing the first two horses where they could not be seen even in daytime because of the trees. He hurried back to his observation place just in time to see the woman leading a second pair out of the gate. It seemed to take a long time before she was back at his side.

"One more to go, but he is being difficult."

"Then forget the horse," he urged.

"It is getting upset because I have taken its friends. I must get the horse or it will begin to raise a big noise."

Longarm knew better than to argue with her about equine behavior, so he bit back a protest and let Keana go back for the last animal, which was now pacing anxiously back and forth in the corral, seeking its companions.

Because the animal was upset, even Keana had trouble getting it bridled. Longarm was taut with anxiety, and then the animal whinnied loudly. One of the horses back in the trees echoed a loud reply.

He saw Keana try to place a hand over the last animal's muzzle to quiet it from whinnying again, but the horse became upset and whirled. Longarm heard a pole splinter, and then the animal bolted through the gate, dragging Keana, who tried to hang on to its reins.

Let go and let's get out of here! Longarm silently pleaded.

The damned horse thundered across the yard, then reversed directions, whinnying for its friends.

Longarm started forward to help Keana just as the door of the cabin flew open and a man in long flannel underwear appeared holding a gun.

"What the hell is going on out here!" he shouted.

Keana struggled to her feet, but she was hurt and only took a few faltering steps before she collapsed.

"Hey!" the outlaw bellowed. "Someone is trying to steal our horses!"

Longarm cursed to himself as men charged outside. He fired at the leader and knocked him down with his first rifle bullet. Levering another shell into the chamber, he just managed to wing a second outlaw before the others returned heavy fire, sending Longarm diving for cover. When he looked up again, all the outlaws were piling back into the shack and they had taken Keana captive.

We're in for it now, he thought bitterly.

A faint light appeared under the closed door, and Longarm could hear the outlaws shouting and cursing. One of them seemed to be in great pain, but that still left three or four others apparently uninjured and madder than hornets. A voice split the night. "Kid, drop that rifle or we're going to kill the woman! We mean it! Come here with your hands in the sky or she's a buzzard bait!"

They think I'm Ta'oie. Should I let them know they're wrong?

"She's alive, kid! Surrender or we'll kill her! You got until I count to ten before I slit her throat!"

Cold sweat erupted across Longarm's body. If he surrendered, both he and Keana would die slowly and painfully. He had killed one of them and wounded a second, so they would not be merciful . . . even to Keana.

I can't stop them from killing her right now if that's what they have in mind . . . but maybe they're bluffing. If they're bluffing, I might be able to do something. Stay free because it's the only chance either of you have to get out of this mess.

The outlaw inside was counting the numbers. He was already at six. "Seven! Eight! I got my knife at her pretty throat now. I mean it, kid. She's gonna die!"

Longarm had to fight an overpowering urge to jump up and surrender. His entire body began to shake and he clenched his fists in frustration, trying desperately not to allow his tortured mind to imagine what was going on inside the mining shack.

"Nine! I'm drawin' blood! You better come out here right now or I'm cuttin' her damn throat!"

"Ten!"

Longarm's heart suddenly felt as if it turned to stone. An anguished sob escaped his throat as he imagined Keana's throat being torn open and blood gushing like a red river down her shirt as she twitched in the throes of an agonizing death.

"She's dead, Injun! *You* killed her!"

Longarm threw back his head and howled at the moon, then reared up on his feet swearing. "You're dead men!" he bellowed. "You're all dead men!"

His outburst must have shaken them badly because several minutes passed before a strained voice replied, "Who are you!"

"I'm your worst nightmare, gawdammit!"

There was a low, hurried murmur of voices, and then: "Who *are* you!"

Longarm didn't know who he was . . . exactly . . . and it didn't matter anyway. They had killed Keana and now they were going to die. He raised his rifle and aimed for a crack in the door, then fired. His slug must have penetrated because he heard a cry of pain, and then the interior of the shack went black.

I'll wait them out and kill them when they have to make a run for food or water, Longarm thought as he took cover and sleeved an icy sweat from his brow. *No mercy for these bloody woman killers, just like they gave none to Keana.*

Chapter 17

Longarm must have dozed off just before dawn because the sound of splintering wood roused him, and then he heard running boots striking the hard ground. Longarm realized that they'd just broken through the rear wall of the shack, then mostly likely divided into two groups. And even though it was too dark to see his enemies, Longarm was quite sure that they intended to catch him in a deadly cross fire.

They'd do it too, if he didn't move fast. But his retreat might already be cut off, so it seemed his best and perhaps only chance was to catch them by surprise and charge the shack. There might still be one or two inside the shack, in which case he'd kill them. With any luck, the others would return and he'd again have the advantage of surprise.

Longarm jumped up and raced toward the shack with his rifle in his left hand and a pistol in his right. Just before he reached the mining shack, its door flew open and a tall man appeared. They both fired at the same instant, but Longarm's bullet did all the damage. The tall man was knocked backward into the shack, and then Longarm was flying through the doorway. The man he'd just wounded was trying to sit up and fire his weapon, but Longarm shot him in the forehead at close range, then ducked to one side as a second outlaw opened fire. Longarm emptied his six-gun at the man and by the time that his hammer dropped on an empty cartridge, both outlaws were dead.

"Keana!"

She was bound and gagged. Her eyes widened with relief when she saw Longarm and she struggled to speak. He hurried over to her side and tore the gag from her mouth. "I thought you were dead," he said.

"Then why'd you come?"

"I didn't have any choice. They caught me napping and I figured I was cut off from my horse and about to be riddled in a cross fire. But I sure am glad they didn't cut your—"

Longarm's words were cut short as a volley of bullets cut through the open doorway. If he and Keana hadn't been on the floor, they'd probably have been hit. He scooted to the door and slammed it shut, then hurried back to Keana as bullets ripped through the thin wooden walls.

"No wonder they ran out of here," Longarm hissed, dragging them both behind a potbellied stove that was the only thing that appeared solid enough to give them any real protection from the bullets ripping through the room. "This place is a death trap!"

"You shouldn't have come. Now we're in even worse shape than we were before."

"I thought you were dead!"

"Never mind that. Untie me and let's see if we can get out the same way that they did."

That sounded good to Longarm. He cut the ropes that bound her wrists and ankles, then glanced at the splintered hole in the back wall. "Let's get out of here!"

They sprinted across the floor of the shack and dove through the wall opening. Then, Longarm grabbed Keana and they raced into the darkness. Two muzzle flashes not twenty-five yards distant reached out for them but missed. Longarm and Keana threw themselves behind a rock that was barely large enough to shield them from gunfire.

"Lanota, do you have any idea where we go from here?"

"None at all."

"We need to get to our horses." Keana shook her head as if to clear it of confusion. "Which way . . ."

"*That* way," he said, pointing toward where most of the gunfire was coming from. "Any other ideas?"

"What do we have to fight them with?"

"One rifle and one pistol. Between the two, I'd guess we have about twenty rounds left. That's not much."

"That's right. And you can bet, if they don't kill us both this morning, one of them will ride off for reinforcements. That's why time is on their side."

Longarm glanced at the sky and knew that daybreak was only a few minutes away. Between now and then, they *had* to cover some ground.

"Then let's go!" Longarm shouted. He jumped up and ran, knowing that Keana was right behind. They sprinted to the side of the canyon, then headed toward its opening, knowing that they had to get out in the open to have any chance of escaping with their lives.

As they approached the canyon's mouth, Longarm ducked behind a rock and whispered, "If I were them, I'd have someone waiting here in ambush."

"Me too, but . . ."

"Just stay put," he ordered.

Longarm holstered his pistol and crept forward with his rifle up and ready. He moved slowly and with great deliberation, even though it was obvious that sunrise was beginning to color the eastern horizon. He almost didn't see the rifleman hiding up in the rocks until it was too late. When the outlaw fired, his shot ricocheted off a rock. Shards of granite peppered Longarm's face, nearly blinding him. But he was able to return fire and kill the ambusher.

"Keana," he shouted. "Come on!"

She raced to his side, and then they were both running out of the canyon. Suddenly in the open, Longarm pulled up short and gasped, "Which way is our best hope?"

"This way," she said, grabbing his hand.

Longarm took a deep breath and wondered if his knee and ankle could stand up to a long, difficult hike across this lonesome country. There was no choice but to try, so he clenched his jaw and they started walking. They didn't travel a mile before they heard the sound of racing hoofbeats and jumped for cover.

"Did they see us?" Keana asked.

"I'm afraid so. Look!"

They raised their heads and saw four horsemen peel off into a circle with the obvious intention of catching them in a noose.

"Damn," Longarm swore helplessly. "We're really in a bad fix now. We'd better find a place to make a stand and do it in a hurry or they'll have us dead in their rifle sights."

"Up there," Keana cried, pointing to a nearby hillock that would at least give them the advantage of shooting down at their enemies.

Longarm gave Keana a hard shove, then unleashed two wild bullets as they began to race up the rocky hillside. The going was tough and they were exposed to a furious volley of gunfire. Dodging and running for their lives, they had almost reached the hilltop when a bullet struck Keana in the shoulder and spun her completely around. Longarm caught her before she hit the ground, but the wound looked bad and the woman collapsed. Longarm scooped her up and somehow made it to the top of the hill, where they had the cover of some rocks.

"I'm hit pretty bad, aren't I?" she whispered, already pale and shaking.

He unbuttoned her shirt and glanced at the ugly bullet wound, knowing it would kill her if he couldn't quickly staunch the severe loss of blood. "You're going to live," he said, only half believing his words. "I'm going to roll you over and see if the bullet passed through your shoulder or not."

"Did it hit my lung?"

They both knew she was a goner for certain if her lung was perforated. "I don't think so. It's a little high, but it probably broke your shoulder. Now just take it easy while I turn you a bit."

Keana was in terrible pain, but she didn't cry out when Longarm eased her onto her side and examined the wound.

"Well?" she asked. "Don't try to fool me, Lanota. Am I finished?"

"You got lucky because the rifle slug passed through your shoulder. That means I just have to get this bleeding stopped and you'll be mustanging again in no time."

Keana managed a weak smile. "I'm not a child, Lanota. We're trapped up here without food or even worse, water. Even if I don't bleed to death, we still haven't got a prayer."

Custis pretended to take offense. "Now that's a real piss-poor attitude!"

"Yeah, but it's true."

"Bullshit! We'll just wait until tonight and sneak off this hill. By morning, we'll be miles away and they'll never find us."

"Thanks for trying to cheer me up, Lanota, but I know I'm going to cash in my chips. But you still have a chance and I want you to take it . . . is that clear!"

"Save your breath," he told her. "I don't want to hear any more of that kind of talk."

Keana grabbed his arm. "Listen to me! I'm feeling weak and dizzy now and I think I'm going to pass out any second."

"Keana, we're going to be okay!"

"But if we're *not*," she replied, "I want you to know that there is gold in that mining shack. Sacks of it that they've looted from the prospector's mine. So, if you make it out alive, maybe you could come back with help and—"

"Hush!" he ordered, ripping off his shirt and then tearing away one of his sleeves. "I'm going to bandage you up good and tight. We'll get this bleeding under control. Then—"

Whatever Longarm had been about to say was instantly forgotten when a rifle slug whined just inches overhead, and then a second came searing in at them from a completely different angle, informing him that the Haskill men were already in position. There was no way out now and it was a long time until nightfall. Maybe too long to offer them any chance of escaping this trap.

"Lanota, one of the men inside that shack who you killed was Eli Haskill," Keana whispered. "But Chance is still out there and he's the smart one."

"What does he look like?"

"He's wearing a blue and red checked shirt. He's a big man, and unless you kill him, you have no chance of escaping. Do you understand? The others are followers. Chance is the one that you have to kill first."

"Then I will." He tore the other sleeve off his shirt. "Now be still or I'll put another gag in your mouth. Is that understood?"

She nodded weakly; then her grip on his arm loosened and she lost consciousness. Fearing that she'd died, Longarm grabbed her wrist and felt for a pulse. It was weak but steady, and he breathed a sigh of relief as he bandaged her wound tightly. The crude bandaging was immediately soaked, but there was nothing else he could do except keep their enemies at bay until dark. Then, if Keana hadn't already bled to death, he'd pick her up and do his damnedest to get them out of this death trap.

But even if they did somehow survive until darkness, Longarm knew that the chances of them both escaping were poor. Keana was right. Without water, food, or horses, they would perish in this badland. *Well, then, I'd better stop thinking of trying to escape and instead be thinking of how to go down there tonight and kill the last four of them one by bloody one. No more running. From this moment on and no matter how absurd it might seem given our desperate situation, I must think that* they *are the hunted, not us.*

Longarm even managed a tight, sardonic smile at the thought that he was in control of things, not Chance Haskill and his three remaining riflemen.

Chapter 18

By late afternoon, Longarm was very thirsty, and suspected that Keana would have been too if she had regained consciousness. Several times that morning, Chance Haskill had ordered his riflemen to open fire in the hope that an errant slug would kill Longarm. The tactic probably would have worked if Custis had not used his knife to carve out a shallow furrow into which he and Keana could press even lower and therefore reduce their chances of getting killed by a ricocheting bullet. After each sustained volley, the Haskill bunch had waited in silence, hoping that Longarm was dead. He'd let them think that and when they'd jumped up and started their charge, he'd opened fire. Now, instead of four Haskill riflemen, there were three.

"Hey!" a voice now called, breaking the stillness. "You interested in seeing another sunrise . . . or do you want to die of thirst?"

"We've got plenty of water in canteens!" Longarm shouted.

"Sure you do!" the man replied in a mocking voice. "And I hate the taste of whiskey! Listen, maybe we can settle this right now between the two of us."

"No, thanks."

"What's the matter, are you afraid of dying quick . . .

161

instead of slow? We'll settle with each other any way you like—with guns, knives, clubs—I don't care! You killed my brother and I am going to kill you!"

"Good luck, Chance," Longarm yelled.

"You're a yellow coward!"

Longarm almost grinned because his response had obviously upset Chance. "Maybe I am. Why don't you rush up here right now and find out."

Several minutes passed with no response. Then Chance screamed, "Who in the hell *are* you?"

Longarm didn't even bother to answer.

"You're not a Ta'oie . . . we know that now. Are you a lawman or just some dumb sonofabitch thinks he can kill my brother and steal our gold?"

"Take your pick," Longarm sang out.

"My imagination tells me that your tongue is swelling up right now and that, by sundown, you'll already be in a terrible thirst."

"Chance, that's amusing because we not only have canteens full of water, but we found a bottle of your whiskey in the mining shack and brought it along to celebrate. That and some of your gold!"

"You lying sonofabitch!" Chance shrieked.

"Whatever you say," Longarm replied, trying to sound cheerful. "But we're happy up here. Hope you and your boys decide to make another rush up the hill. I'd enjoy killing all you Haskill sonofabitches before sundown."

"You're bluffing!"

"Try me," Longarm replied.

"The woman is dead! I saw her fall."

"She's alive and well."

"Then let's hear her."

"Nope. She's taking a nap, Chance. Gonna be wide awake tonight when you and your friends come calling."

Longarm raised up in the desperate hope that he could see at least the top of Chance Haskill's head and then blow it off, but the man was staying low.

"Speaking of friends," Chance finally said, "I got some coming. And I'm going to tell them I want you taken alive tonight. Know why?"

"I can guess."

"No, you can't," Chance shouted. "You have no idea of the torture that I'm going to put you through for killing Eli and the others. If you had any brains, you'd blow them out right now. Only, I keep forgetting that you are having a good time with Keana's body up there. Ain't that right!"

Longarm didn't trust himself to answer, so he hunkered down in the rocks and waited. Chance kept up the baiting for another half hour before he began shouting vile curses.

"Lanota?"

He glanced down at Keana. "You woke up just in time to listen to Chance tell me how I was violating your lovely body."

"You know what he's trying to do."

"Yeah. But we're not buying into that, and when darkness comes, I'm going down this hill to finish them off. There are only three left and I can take them. We're going to get out of this and you'll see Ta'oie again . . . along with your mustangs. So don't give up, Keana."

"I won't," she promised.

Longarm resumed sucking on the little pebble he'd put in his mouth several hours earlier. He gazed up at the sun and reckoned he'd be settling a score with Chance and the others in just a couple of more hours. Actually, he could hardly wait.

"Keana?"

The sun was going down and it was time to get ready to do or die. Longarm leaned close to the woman and whispered again in her ear. "Keana, I need you to wake up now. Can you hear me?"

Her lips moved and her eyelids fluttered. Longarm checked her pulse, and it was steady but weak. Although the bleeding had finally stopped, she'd already lost far too much blood and he knew that she could die of shock.

163

"I have to go down and face them," he told her. "I'll use the rifle. You keep the pistol. If they manage to get past me, then defend yourself. Do you understand what I'm saying?"

The eyes opened and gazed up at him. "Yes."

"Good," he replied, giving her the weapon. "Take this pistol and hang on to it tight. I won't be gone long."

Keana curled her finger around the trigger so that Longarm knew she understood.

"That's my girl," he said. "When I return, I'll sing out so you don't plug me by mistake. But if you hear someone and they don't call out, don't hesitate to put a bullet into them."

"All right."

Longarm smoothed her brow. "I tell you something," he said, giving the sun a few more minutes to disappear and the light to fade completely. "If I loved mustangs as much as you and Ta'oie, I'd stick around in this country and the first thing I'd do is make you my bride. I mean that, Keana. You're a hell of a fine woman. So maybe, if I can pull this off, we can still do something together on permanent basis."

"You'd marry me?"

He smiled. "Yeah."

"Then I think I'm going to make it," she said slowly. "You won't change your mind, will you?"

"Nope, and you've my word on it. If we pull this off and manage to get back to civilization, we'll get hitched in Denver."

"That's the best offer I've ever had."

"Keep it mind."

"Oh, I won't forget. Hold me for a minute, Lanota, then kiss me good-bye."

"My pleasure," he said, fighting off tears.

A few minutes later, Longarm picked up his rifle, glanced up at the rising moon, and then slithered through the rocks like a rattlesnake and was gone. He moved slowly and without a sound. His preference was to kill Chance

Haskill first and see if the others still had a mind to fight. But there was no way of knowing exactly where to find Chance, so he'd kill the first man that he could find.

Ten minutes later, he froze on the rocky ground and saw a shadow of motion. Longarm pulled the rifle up and took aim. He held his breath, wanting a little more definition in his target, and when that happened, he aimed for the man's upper body and squeezed off a shot.

The result was both immediate and gratifying. Longarm saw the figure lift up in the air and slam down on its back. He heard a strangled curse and then a death rattle.

"Jud!" Chance shouted from somewhere in the darkness off to Longarm's left side. "Jud, did you get him!"

"Yeah," Longarm grunted.

"Nice goin'!" another voice called.

Longarm heard the pounding of boots and levered another shell into the chamber of his rifle, then waited a few seconds until a second man appeared. He skidded to a halt, then saw Longarm's outline on the ground.

"Jud?" the fellow said. "Jud, is that you!"

"Afraid not," Longarm said a moment before he drilled the man with a clean shot through the heart.

A muzzle flash off to Longarm's left told him that Chance wasn't going to be as easy to kill. Longarm returned fire, then rolled several times as bullets sought him out. He waited for a target and when there was none, he held his breath, finger on the trigger.

But Chance Haskill had something else in mind. Longarm could hear the pounding of his boots as he raced up the hill.

"Keana, look out!" he shouted, firing several blind shots in helpless frustration.

Chance's silhouette stood out clearly for an instant when he reached the crest of the hill and gazed down at Keana. Then, Longarm saw the man lift his gun and point it at the woman.

Longarm unleashed a desperate shot upward, and at the same instant Keana fired her pistol. Chance staggered and Longarm saw the flash of his muzzle blast, and then unleashed a second round at the tall, swaying figure.

Chance screamed and toppled. He struck the ground and rolled down the hillside to stop not fifty feet from where Longarm was standing. Longarm was taking no chances, so he shot the outlaw leader once more just to make sure Chance was really dead. Then he hurried back up the hill.

"Lanota here!" he yelled breathlessly.

The click of a pistol's hammer told him that if he'd forgotten to call out, he'd be as dead as Chance Haskill.

"Keana!" He lay down beside her. "We did it!"

"Yes," she whispered. "And now I'm going to live and marry you, my darling."

Longarm held her tight. Soon, he would walk back down the hill and gather canteens, guns, food, and yes . . . even a dead man's gold.

"Lanota, you won't go back on your word, will you?"

"Never."

"Are there any mustangs running wild near Denver?"

"I doubt it."

"What about in the Rockies?"

"Maybe."

"If there are, we'll find them," she promised.

"Yeah." He took a deep breath. "But what about Ta'oie?"

"He'll come with us . . . or not. It will be up to him."

"Sure."

Keana hugged him with more strength than he had thought she could possibly possess. "I am *so* happy now!"

"Me too. I thought we might be goners."

"I knew you would kill them all."

"But I didn't. You killed Chance."

"Yes. I had already forgotten."

He cradled Keana in his arms a while longer before she drifted back into either sleep or unconsciousness, and then Longarm walked slowly back down the hill.

Chapter 19

Longarm sat basking in the afternoon sun with his chair tipped back against the mining shack. An entire restful week had passed since his deadly showdown with Chance and the notorious Haskill Gang. During that period, Longarm had explored the mine, and it was clear that it had been worked out and offered no more gold. By the lantern light, he could see where a small but rich vein of ore had run nearly twenty feet back into the mine before it petered out.

Longarm didn't really care because they had six bags of extremely high-grade ore resting in the cabin just waiting to be transported to Denver, then assayed and auctioned off to the highest bidder. Longarm guessed that each bag weighed about fifteen pounds, and although there was a good deal of quartz mixed in with the gold, he figured that their combined value would exceed five thousand dollars; a small fortune by almost anyone's standards.

Of much greater concern was restoring Keana's fragile health and getting her back on her feet. She'd lost so much blood and strength that Longarm knew it would probably kill the woman to travel, so they would wait and spend however much time it took before leaving this cabin.

"Lanota?" her voice called from inside.

Longarm's eyes popped open and the front legs of his

chair struck the ground. He'd been dozing again, regaining his own strength.

"Yeah?"

"Come in and talk to me awhile."

Longarm ambled into the mining shack, which now appeared far different than it had on the murderous night when he'd burst inside and killed two outlaws, then rescued Keana. He'd cleaned out all the filth and trash left by the Haskill Gang and burned it in the yard. He'd washed the bedding and scrubbed the kitchen pots and pans, then cooked a bit of beans and salt pork. He'd even baked some bread, and shot a careless mule deer to add to their larder. Now, the place was fit to live in while they convalesced.

"How you doing?" he asked, sitting down beside Keana and taking her hand.

"Better every day."

"Your color is much improved." Longarm peeled back her blanket and then gently removed a clean bandage from her bullet-riddled shoulder. "It's healing just fine. Now roll over and let me take a peek at the exit wound."

Keana frowned and eyed him with suspicion. "I'm not sure that I can trust you ever again. Last time, you really goosed me with your thumb!"

"I apologize. Really, I just couldn't help myself."

"Dammit," Keana said accusingly, "it wasn't all that funny!"

"No more goosing." Longarm had to struggle to keep a straight face. "Keana, I promise."

"Okay."

The bullet's exit wound was also healing nicely, although it was much larger and uglier. Longarm was glad that Keana couldn't see the amount of permanent scarring that it would leave along with a very evident depression. But the truth was, the woman had every reason to consider herself extremely fortunate to be alive.

"How does it look?" she asked.

"It will take a while longer to heal, but I see no sign of

infection. You're going to be up and about soon."

"I sure hope so, but I still feel weak."

"You lost a lot of blood. It takes time."

"I suppose." Keana's voice hardened. "I hated those men and I'm glad that you killed them all. When I think about how we were up against eight men . . . well, I can scarcely believe we survived."

He blinked and stared. "Did you say eight?"

"Yes."

Longarm jumped to his feet. "Keana, there was Eli and that other fella I shot when I burst in here . . . and then that ambusher that I killed outside this shack. Then there was Chance and the other three with him that last night when we were making our stand on the hill. It adds up to seven and that's how many I buried last week."

She looked away for a moment, and he could see her lips move as she silently counted the number of outlaws who had been with Chance.

"Well?" he asked impatiently.

In a small voice, she said, "Lanota, one got away."

Longarm fought down a wave of panic. "Do you think he was the last of the gang who was just trying to save his own hide . . . or did he go for reinforcements?"

"I don't know. There are a bunch of Haskills, but I'm not sure exactly how many are still alive and in these parts. And besides, you and Sheriff Benton might have killed a few more."

"I'd guess, but I can't tell you for certain."

She looked him in the eye. "So what are we going to do?"

"Make tracks as fast as we can," he told her without hesitation. "There's a buckboard out in the yard and we have plenty of horses. I'll hitch a couple to the wagon, turn the others loose, and we'll head for our mustang camp. We can collect Ta'oie and his mustangs, then just hope we reach Elko without any more fighting."

"It would be a lot faster if we left the buckboard here and rode the horses."

"You're in no shape for that," he told her, already thinking about what he'd need to load in the wagon. "I'll place the bedding in the wagon for you to rest upon."

"Lanota, if we do run into some of the last members of the gang, I think we ought to have a relay team of horses saddled and bridled. We could outrun another bunch of Haskills."

"What about the gold?"

"I've no intention of leaving it behind for the likes of those vicious animals."

Longarm could see that argument was out of the question. Keana was willing to die, if necessary, rather than hand over the gold. "Okay," he agreed. "I'll hitch two horses to the buckboard and saddle another four."

She sat up and reached for her shirt. "Please let me try and help."

"Listen. Your wounds are not healed and they could re-open if you move too much or too fast."

"But—"

"Keana, you've got to trust me! For reasons even I can't explain, I seem to know all about bullet wounds. I'm saying that you're not in any shape to ride a horse, lift so much as a bag of that gold ore, or move around unless it is absolutely necessary."

"But don't you see—maybe it *is* necessary that I do all those things!"

"And maybe not," he sternly reminded her. "We don't know for sure what happened to the eighth man. He might have grabbed several bags of gold and made a run for his life. But if he went for more Haskill men, we have to be ready to fight again. And you can't possibly help me in a gun battle if those wounds reopen and you're bleeding all over the wagon."

Her fists clenched in frustration, but Keana said, "Okay, you win. I'll stay right here and watch you pack and I promise I won't try to help, but I sure won't let you forget the gold. I'm counting on it for Ta'oie's surgery."

"Fair enough." Longarm headed for the door. "I'll see if I can find the harness and get that buckboard hitched. Then I'll drive it up near this shack and we'll start loading the bed and finally . . . . you."

"Good! But dammit, I sure hate to just lie here like a worthless nothing while you do all the work."

"I can handle it. We'll be out of here in less than an hour, if the buckboard is sound and the harness isn't rotten."

"And the horses cooperate."

"Yeah, that too."

Longarm hurried outside to the buckboard. He'd passed it twenty times or more this last week, but he hadn't paid it any mind. Now, however, he examined the wagon with a critical eye, and was relieved to discover that it was serviceable. He also found a set of harness in the back of the wagon that appeared to be very worn and in questionable condition, but he knew that it would have to suffice. If something broke, Longarm reckoned that he could rig replacement leathers that would hold up until they reached Elko or some ranch where they could buy a better set of harness.

The outlaw horses were not mustangs, so he chose a large, complacent-looking pair of bay geldings, and had no difficulty harnessing them to the buckboard. Things seemed to be going well as he drove the wagon to the front of the mining shack, then tied the animals to the porch and burst inside.

"What are you doing out of bed!" he shouted in anger.

"I had to get dressed, didn't I?" She glared back at him. "Or did you think I was going to make my entrance into Elko stark naked?"

Longarm grumbled, but helped her pull on her boots, then buckle her belt. She'd already rigged up a sling and found her hat.

"I hate to be a wet blanket, Lanota, but just how are you supposed to get that bed through the narrow door?"

He frowned, "Hmm, now that could be a problem."

"Forget the bed and just throw that old straw mattress in the back of the wagon. Then help me up and I'll handle the rest."

"Sounds good."

Longarm dragged the bedding outside and heaved it into the buckboard. Then he helped Keana across the room and outside to the wagon, and gently lifted her onto the soft mattress and blankets. "Are you all right?"

"I will be as soon as you hand me those bags of gold ore."

"Sure! And we'll take all the weapons I removed from the bodies as well as the food. I'll fill all the canteens, saddle the four horses, and then I believe we'll be ready to roll."

Keana sat up and looked all around. "I won't mind putting this canyon and mining shack far behind us. There's been a lot of blood spilled here. Unfortunately, some of it was mine."

Longarm got their four reserve horses saddled and bridled, then tied them to the back of the wagon where Keana could watch them.

"Are you ready!" he called, lighting a match and pitching it inside the mining shack, which he'd liberally doused with kerosene.

"Let's go!" she answered.

Custis gave the horses a flick on their backs with the lines and got them moving away from the cabin. He passed seven shallow and unmarked graves. The shack caught on fire, and was burning furiously by the time they were out of the canyon. Longarm glanced back at Keana, who was watching the rising flames with tears in her dark eyes. He didn't even want to think about the outrages Chance Haskill and his outlaws had no doubt committed against poor

172

Keana before he'd come to her rescue. The hell with that because he'd still be more than proud to marry her in Denver . . . if they ever got out of this hellish mustanging country alive.

Chapter 20

Although Longarm had a persistent and very uneasy feeling that the lone survivor of the Haskill Gang had gone for help, he told himself that it was more likely that the man had simply run for his life and would never return. This would be even more likely if he'd somehow managed to escape with a sack or two or gold ore.

Would I come back after seeing most of my friends killed in a shootout? This was the question that Longarm asked himself time and time again as the first day passed.

He drove the buckboard slowly, partly because the terrain was so rough and slashed with deep arroyos that had to be skirted, but also because he did not want to take any chance that Keana's shoulder wound would reopen.

"Lanota," she complained, "at this rate, it's going to take us forever to find Ta'oie and our mustangs."

"I know, I know," he replied. "But this buckboard isn't in the greatest shape, and if we should break a spoke and lose a wheel—or worse—we'd be a in bad fix."

"No, we wouldn't. We'd just load the gold ore onto a couple of the extra horses and ride. I think that's what we need to do anyway."

"I disagree."

"Damn but you're the bossy one! What makes you think that you can make all the decisions?"

"I'm the driver," he said, smothering a smile. "You're just along for the ride."

"The hell I am! I'm the one that knows and loves this country. You don't even know where the next water hole is to be found."

"You're right," he admitted. "So why don't you tell me so these horses can drink their fill tonight."

Keana muttered something Longarm didn't particularly think he wanted to hear, then said, "Angle us more to the southwest. There's a spring up ahead about three miles that will do just fine."

"Thank you."

They bumped along in silence for another mile. Then Keana said, "We're going to take Ta'oie to Denver for surgery. Right?"

"That's the plan."

"So are we getting married before or after the operation?"

"I hadn't thought much about that. Which would you prefer?"

"Seems like we'd be a little preoccupied with worrying and watching over Ta'oie to enjoy a honeymoon."

"You're right," he said, twisting to speak directly to her. "We would be. That settles it. We'll get married when Ta'oie is up and around."

"Okay. What's Denver like?"

"I have no recollection."

"Do you have any idea what you did or where we'll live in Denver?"

Longarm turned back around when the buckboard's front wheel bounced over a large rock and nearly threw him out of his seat. He'd have to keep his eyes on the business of driving. "Keana, I must have lived someplace in the city."

"What did you do for a living?"

"I have no idea. Perhaps I was a merchant or a wagon driver."

"From what I've seen today, that's impossible."

"Thanks."

"I sure would hate to live in a city much bigger than Elko, and Denver is probably a *lot* larger."

"That wouldn't surprise me."

"Lanota? Have you ever wondered if you have a wife and family?"

He spun around and gawked at her.

"Well?" she asked, looking up at him. "What if you do? We can't be married if you already are married. That would make you a bigamist, and only the Mormon men can get away with that."

"I might *be* a Mormon bigamist, for all we know." Longarm decided to enjoy this conversation. "You wouldn't mind sharing me with a couple of other wives, now would you?"

"Sure I would! What kind of a fool question is that anyhow!"

"Don't get your drawers in a dither."

"Well, I just never heard of such a thing. Here we are supposed to get married and we're just now discussing the very real possibility that you are *already* married and might have a whole bunch of children waiting in Denver for their long-lost daddy."

They rode along in silence for another mile. Then Longarm said, "So what would you like to do if I am a family man?"

"I don't know."

"Tell you what. We'll go to Denver and if I am married and have a bunch of brats, then we'll just leave town and live somewhere else."

"You'd *abandon* your wife and kids!" She sounded horrified.

"Why not? We're in love. But I guess that . . ." He let his doubtful voice trail off into silence.

177

"You guess what?"

"Well, if my wife was rich or especially beautiful, then I'd have to think twice about leaving her."

"Then what would I do!"

"You could still be my loving little Mustang Maiden and I'd keep you someplace. Find a little room in a tenement building. Of course, I'd expect you to work and earn your keep. But I'd come around as often as I possibly could. Honest."

"I'd *hate* living like that!"

"Keana, why don't we stop jumping to conclusions and just wait and see if I'm married and have a bunch of kids? I'm sure when I get to Denver that all of my past will become clear as crystal."

"Yeah," she agreed, sounding worried. "I suppose it will. You might be single . . . though I doubt it because you're a big, handsome dog. Some woman must have snapped you up years ago."

"I'm not wearing a wedding band."

"Maybe it was stolen by the Haskills or you lost it or you . . . you wouldn't take it off to fool me into believing you were a single man, would you?"

"I doubt it, honey."

"Humph!"

By the time they arrived at the springs, Keana was even more upset. She barely allowed him to help her out of the buckboard and then over to a place where she could rest.

"I'll water the horses, then come back and cook us something to eat," he promised. "You rest easy."

She nodded in stern silence and watched as he took each of their horses and let them drink their fills before he hobbled them so they could graze on what little grass there was to be found.

"You'd best leave those four animals saddled!" she called. "Just in case we get jumped."

"I don't think that there is much chance of that," he

yelled back. "I haven't seen a sign of life for miles and miles all around."

"Yeah, but this land can fool you. An entire wagon train could be camped just over that ridge yonder and we'd never know it."

Longarm nodded, but he removed the saddles and bridles anyway. He didn't like the way she was trying to tell him what to do . . . no, he didn't care for it even a little bit. And despite the fun he'd had at her expense earlier, he was starting to wonder if he really could be married with children. If he was, Longarm sure hoped the woman was good-natured and pretty and that his kids were respectful. Kids could be terrors and a nagging woman was always a trial.

Stop it, he told himself. *I'd remember if I were married . . . I'm almost sure of that much.*

Still, "almost" wasn't entirely good enough, and they both fretted about that until darkness fell.

"Good night," Longarm said after checking her shoulder bandage. "I guess we'll hook up with Ta'oie sometime tomorrow."

"We should reach that canyon where we trapped the sorrel stallion's band of mustangs by early afternoon. Ta'oie will be waiting and the seven mustangs will be tamed and ready to ride."

"But we don't really need to sell them now, do we?" he asked. "I mean, with all the money that ore will bring in Denver, we could turn them loose."

"Sure," she agreed, "but we won't."

"Why not?"

"Because now that they're gentled to human touch, they're ruined for the wild. Don't you know that all wild things that are tamed lose their wildness?"

"I hadn't thought much about it one way or the other."

"Well," she said, "it's true. Those seven mustangs would go back to their band, but they'd still be saddle horses. And most likely, some sonofabitchin' mustanger would come along and catch 'em. Then, because he wouldn't really be able to understand horses, he'd ship them out in boxcars for dog food. Now, wouldn't that be a terrible waste?"

"Sure would be." Longarm frowned. "All right, then we'll take them to Elko and sell them as saddle horses because you can *never* have too much money."

"Oh," she replied, "I don't know about that. I've heard that the railroad barons are the richest men in America and all of them are robbers and thieves. And I know a few rich ranchers that are as crooked as a dog's hind leg. I've heard it said before that money and power will corrupt a person every time."

"We won't be that rich," he told her. "And I'm not sure that I wouldn't mind a little corrupting."

"Lanota, don't talk stupid!" She sat up and stared through the twilight at him. "I can't believe that you'd actually leave your family."

"Why not, if we're in love?"

Keana made an very uncomplimentary sound. "You sure talk crazy for being an honorable man."

"Who says I'm honorable?"

"I do, because you risked your life to save mine. That's honorable. But then you tell me you'd leave a good wife and children."

"I'd only leave a wife if she was poor, crabby, or ugly. If she was any of those things, I'd leave her fast enough to make her head spin."

"Don't say anything more," Keana warned. "You're getting yourself deeper and deeper into the manure pile."

"Huh?"

"Go to sleep, Lanota. Let's just pretend that we haven't had this conversation and I didn't hear you say you'd ever leave your wife and kids."

He lay back on his blanket and allowed himself a big grin. Longarm didn't know what he had left behind in Denver, but now he was quite sure that he did not want to get married.

• • •

They didn't have much of anything nice to say to each other the next morning. Longarm harnessed and saddled the horses, then transferred Keana back to the wagon.

"Here we go," he said. "Hang on tight."

"Don't need to do that, given how you've been driving this thing like an old lady with a couple of big boils on her butt!"

"Keana, honey, you're getting ornerier by the hour."

"Just drive and leave me in peace. I'm still mad about you admitting you'd abandon your wife and kids."

"I may not even have any!"

"No matter. You've shown me a side of yourself that I didn't see before."

Longarm was getting steamed and the fun had definitely worn thin. So he kept his silence all morning as they crossed the desert basin. He was skirting a deep wash and paying very close attention to his wheels when a man with a double-barreled shotgun suddenly leaped out from behind a rock, pointed the rifle at his head, and shouted, "Stop or I'll blow your damned brains out!"

Longarm wasn't a fool and he did exactly as he was told. At this close range, the outlaw could not possibly have missed.

"Keana," the wild-looking man with long black hair screamed, "raise your hands so that I can see them and get your pretty ass out of that wagon. Try anything funny and I'll blow both your heads off!"

"She can't raise her arms," Longarm argued. "Not with a hole in her right shoulder."

"Shut up! Remove that pistol with your left hand, then climb down from that wagon real slow, Marshal Long."

Longarm blinked with surprise. "My name is Marshal Long?"

"Don't play stupid!"

"I'm really a marshal?"

"One more word and you're a *dead* federal marshal."

Longarm unholstered his gun, then pitched it into the

sage. He climbed down and started to go back to the wagon and help Keana, but the outlaw shrieked, "Stay away from her. Spread-eagle in the dirt!"

"Okay," Longarm said, desperately trying to think of some way to save himself and Keana. "Just . . . just take it easy."

"Well," the outlaw said, turning his attention to Keana. "You really *are* in bad shape."

"Yeah, Orvis," Keana replied, "but your brothers are *both* dead."

"As you will be soon enough."

"What are you going to do?" Longarm asked. "If it's the gold that you want . . . then take all of it."

"Don't worry, I will." Orvis Haskill marched over to Keana and without warning or hesitation, punched her wounded shoulder with the shotgun. Keana sobbed and her knees buckled as Orvis struck her again in the same shoulder.

Longarm started to jump up, but Orvis swung his shotgun around and hissed, "Stop right there or I'll blow your head off!"

Keana's face was white with pain. Longarm could see fresh blood already starting to soak through her bandage. He was trembling with rage, and it was all he could do not to attack in the vain hope that he might be able to get ahold of Orvis and somehow kill him before being blown in half by the shotgun.

"How does it feel to finally be on the losing end?" Orvis taunted him. "We killed Sheriff Benton but we never quite got rid of you, and that was our big mistake."

"Glad to hear it."

"Yeah, but ain't it funny how a thing that at first seems like bad luck turns out just the opposite? If my horse hadn't gone lame yesterday afternoon, I wouldn't be here to relieve you of those ore sacks and then have the pleasure of settling the score."

182

"Life," Longarm drawled, "is just full of happy surprises."

"But not for you today, Marshal Custis Long. When we first heard that they'd sent you all the way from Denver to put our heads in hangman's nooses, we thought it was a joke. Chance about died laughing, and so did me and Eli."

"But then you found out the joke was on yourselves, didn't you?" Longarm said, finally remembering exactly how it had ended for poor Sheriff Benton.

"Yeah," Orvis admitted. "We stopped laughing. But guess who is about to start laughing right now?"

"You?"

"Right! And I sure wish my brothers and the rest of the gang could see what I'm going to do to you both next."

Longarm felt his skin prickle with dread, but managed to grin and say, "I suppose it's not going to be real pleasant, huh?"

"It will be for me. Marshal Long, I never killed a federal officer before, so I'm going to do it slow and teach you everything you'll ever learn about suffering and pain." He glanced down at Keana, hunger burning in his eyes. "And you . . . well, we're going to have some fun on that mattress up in the wagon. Lots of fun before I'm satisfied."

"You'd better kill me quick," she sobbed, "because I'll find a way to kill you, so help me!"

"Big talk for a woman who looks like death warmed over," Orvis mocked. He turned back to Longarm. "Put your hands behind your back and put your face into the dirt."

"Go to Hell!"

"No," Orvis said with a terrible laugh, "I believe I'll send you there instead."

Longarm saw the man's finger tighten on the trigger and he braced himself. But then, the boom of a rifle shot exploded. Orvis reared back on his boot heels and pitched over backward, dead before he struck the ground.

"Hey!" a shrill voice called. "It's Ta'oie!"

Longarm expelled a deep sigh of relief, then crawled over to Keana and pressed his hand against her shoulder wound. "You're an amazing woman. I didn't think you had anymore blood left."

"Me neither. Can you . . . can you stop it? I'm already feeling weak."

Longarm nodded. "You didn't survive all this to die now. So hang on because you're going to live to see Ta'oie walk tall in Denver."

"I know," she whispered. "But I'm not sure that I still want to get married or live in some tenement."

"Don't worry about that now. Just rest easy."

Keana closed her eyes, and Longarm wasted no time in changing her bandage, knowing that she would survive.

We all will, Longarm thought as the Paiute boy hobbled over to his side and stared down at the Mustang Maiden.

"Lanota, is she going to die!"

"Not a chance."

Unbidden tears spilled out of the Paiute kid's eyes and he roughly sleeved them dry. "I love Keana."

"I know. And she loves you."

"But she loves you *more,* Lanota."

"Not more . . . just in a different way. And anyway, for what it is worth, there's no doubt now in my mind that she'll still be here mustanging with you long, long after I've gone."

Ta'oie grinned and laid his hand on Longarm's broad shoulder. "You are a good friend. A good man too."

"So are you," Longarm told him, "and one day you're going to walk tall and proud and be a leader of your people."

Chapter 21

When the surgeon emerged from his operating room, Long-arm and Keana both pivoted around at the same instant.

"Relax," the Denver physician said. "Ta'oie's operation was an unqualified success. We had to break the ankle and reset it, and I'm not saying that his recovery and rehabilitation won't be slow and painful, but the boy ought to walk and run just as he did before the accident."

"Thank heavens!" Keana cried.

"Yes," Longarm said. "He's a good kid."

"I'm sure that he is," the surgeon replied. "And he has a remarkable tolerance for pain."

"Whatever we owe you will be fully paid," Longarm promised.

"Five hundred for me and a few hundred more for the hospital. I'm sure it won't add up to a thousand dollars. What will happen to Ta'oie?"

"He'll go back to Nevada and his people," Keana answered. "Ta'oie would never fit into city living."

"No," the doctor said, "I suppose not. Well, I'll talk to you later. Keana, how is that shoulder?"

"It's just fine."

"Let me be the judge of that when I examine you tomorrow. All right?"

"Sure."

The surgeon turned and left them in the hospital corridor. Longarm was grinning from ear to ear. "I think that Ta'oie would like to see you immediately," he said.

"You too."

"I'll wait a few minutes and then come in," Longarm promised.

Keana hurried into the little room reserved for post-surgical patients. Longarm lit a cigar and stared out the hospital window, thinking. He was so engrossed in his thoughts that he didn't hear her return.

"Ta'oie wants to see you now . . . alone."

Longarm jammed his cigar in a bucket of sand and went in to see the kid. Ta'oie was pale but smiling. "The doctor says you'll run like a deer one day," Longarm told him.

"Thank you, Lanota."

"You're more than welcome." Longarm's brow furrowed. "Ta'oie, I've got some bad news. I haven't told this to Keana yet but . . . well, I got a wife and six kids living a few miles south of town."

"A wife?"

"Yep. She's not as pretty as Keana, but she loves me and I can't leave her."

"Six children? Six little Lanotas?" Ta'oie's eyes grew wide with amazement.

"That's right. I'm afraid it means that I won't be able to marry Keana. I know she'll feel awful and want to go back to mustanging. So I want you to be, well . . . just help her all that you can."

"Me?"

"That's right," Longarm said gravely. "You'll do that, won't you?"

Ta'oie couldn't help but smile. "I will!"

"That's good. Very good!"

Then, for reasons that neither understood, they both started laughing.

Watch for

LONGARM AND THE DYNAMITE DAMSEL

256th novel in the exciting LONGARM series
from Jove

Coming in March!

LONGARM

Explore the exciting Old West with one of the men who made it wild!